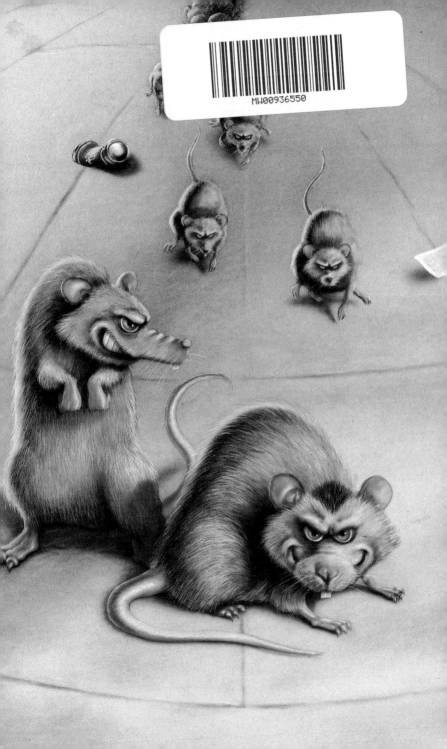

Creatures

See How They Run

He spun round. Behind him, on the floor, were six very large rats. They were sitting up on their haunches, front paws raised, staring at him.

Then he saw eight more in the doorway. These were smaller – more like normal size – but they were sitting up, too. Very still. Very quiet. *Staring*.

Jon swallowed. He moved the torch – and there were more rats, on a fallen beam that lay at a sloping angle between the ceiling and the floor. Lined in a row, sitting up, and absolutely motionless as they watched with their mean, beady little eyes.

The ugly truth dawned on Jon even before he started to swing the torch around in a wide arc. There were rats everywhere.

Creatures

See How They Run

Louise Cooper

Scholastic Children's Books
Commonwealth House, 1–19 New Oxford Street,
London WC1A 1NU, UK
London ~ New York ~ Toronto ~ Sydney ~ Auckland
Mexico City ~ New Delhi ~ Hong Kong

First published by Scholastic Ltd, 1998

ISBN 0 590 54381 4

Typeset by Falcon Oast Graphic Art
Printed by Cox & Wyman Ltd., Reading, Berks

10 9 8 7 6 5 4 3

1

"What do you reckon, Gnash?" Jon said as they both looked out of the window at the garden of their new home. "Looks all right, doesn't it? Plenty of places for you to explore."

Gnasher had his front paws on the sill and his back paws on a packing case. His ears were pricked forward and his black-and-white plume of a tail waved, the way it always did when he saw something intriguing. Then he meowed. It was the kind of meow that suggested, "Never mind the talk, let me get out there!"

"OK, in a minute." The garden was a mess, Jon thought, but that would suit Gnasher fine.

Suit him, as well. When he'd found out that his family would have to share the garden with the people in the downstairs half of the house, he'd groaned inwardly, imagining some neat and prissy exhibition piece where he'd get yelled at if he went within ten metres of a flower-bed and football was right out of the question. But obviously the neighbours weren't into gardening, *and* they had a son of about Jon's age. This place wasn't going to be bad at all.

"Jon!" His older sister, Gina's, voice called from another room. "Have you gone to sleep in there? Come on, Dad wants a hand lugging some more stuff!"

"Coming!" It didn't look as if the boy downstairs was going to appear; it was Saturday, so he was probably out. Jon wondered, briefly, what lay beyond the line of scrubby trees on the other side of the low garden wall, then tore himself away from the window. Gnasher jumped down too, tail in the air now. He headed for the kitchen (typical cat, Jon thought) and Jon went reluctantly off to help with the lugging.

Dinner that evening was a take-away from a Chinese up the road, and they ate it in the middle of chaos, sitting on the living-room floor with a crate for a table.

"At least everything's in," Mum said cheerfully when Dad grumbled about the mess. "We'll straighten up tomorrow."

Jon pushed Gnasher's inquiring nose away from his king prawns and pineapple. "My room's great," he said. "Looks out over the garden. Dad, what's on the other side of the wall? Behind those trees?"

Dad raised his eyebrows. "As if I'd had a chance to look!"

"It's a railway cutting," said Gina. "All overgrown; I shouldn't think the railway's been used for years. Mum, I don't see why Jon should have that bedroom. Mine's *tiny*, and it doesn't get any sunlight!"

"I bagged it first," Jon retorted. "Anyway," he looked pointedly at Gina's black leggings, black sweatshirt and heavy black eye makeup (her hair was black this week, too), "vampires don't want sunlight. It kills 'em."

"Well, I'd rather be a vampire than a slimy, punky little—"

3

"Shut up, the pair of you!" said Dad. "If you want to argue about it, do it when I'm not around, all right? And Jon, if you let that cat eat off your plate—"

Jon gave Gnasher a shove. "Get *off*, Gnasher! You've got your own Kitty-Slurp in the kitchen!"

Gnasher gave him a filthy look and went off in a huff. He jumped on to the windowsill and sat staring out. His tail twitched. Then he raised one paw and patted at the glass.

"He wants to go out," said Gina. "Can he, Mum?"

"No, love, not till tomorrow; and not at night at all until he learns his way around. Otherwise he might go off exploring and get lost."

"I've seen loads of other cats round here," Gina observed. "Plenty for him to make friends with."

Jon knew that any cat who tried to "make friends" with Gnasher usually ended up with a clawed nose, bitten ears and clumps of fur missing. Gnasher was a total softie with people, but saw anything on four legs as a deadly enemy to be beaten or eaten, or both. Cats, mice, birds, even dogs four times his size

4

– Gnasher wasn't afraid of anything. He'd probably tackle a rhinoceros if he ever met one.

Ignoring a frustrated growl from the cat – who was now trying to work out how to open the window – Jon asked, "Has anyone met the people downstairs yet?"

"The Lamberts?" Dad helped himself to more fried rice. "I saw them earlier and we said hello. They seem OK. Their boy's called Frankie."

"What's he like?"

"Oh . . . small, dark, a bit on the thin side. Quiet, I'd say."

"Quiet? Some hope!" Gina muttered under her breath. Jon stuck his tongue out at her.

"And before you ask, Jon, I've no idea which team Frankie supports," Dad added with a grin. "Could be Spurs, for all I know."

"Oh, ha, ha!" Jon was an Arsenal fan, which was just as well, now that they were living in North London.

He scraped the last bits from his foil dish and savoured them. "Mmm. Good. Is there any more?"

"No, but I bought some cakes from that all-night place on the corner," Mum told him.

"Only one each, mind. Then you and Gina can help me get the duvets out and make up the beds. I'm going to sleep like a corpse tonight, and I bet you will too."

It was a pity he hadn't taken Mum up on her bet, Jon thought later, because it was long past midnight now, and he was still wide awake.

Part of it, of course, was simply the fact of being in a new and strange place. Everything looked weird, from the shape of the room to the way the moonlight came in at the window, and all the familiar furniture was in the wrong places. And it wasn't quiet, the way their old house in the suburbs had been. They were close to the heart of London here, and the noise of traffic was a distant but constant hum. Even from the back of the house, where his room was, Jon could hear street noises. Voices laughed and shouted now and then, and half an hour ago a car had gone down the road with its stereo thumping out a huge bass beat. Jon liked the noise. It made the city feel alive, and even here in his room he could be part of that life. He could lie here all night, he thought, and just listen.

Someone else seemed to feel the same way. Gnasher was perched on the windowsill, staring out into the dark. His ears flicked and swivelled, and every few seconds his tail would twitch as if with excitement. The cat was *fascinated* by the garden! Probably he could see things out there that human eyes couldn't. Mice, hedgehogs – there might even be a fox prowling through the night. Funny to think of wild animals like foxes in the middle of the city. . .

Suddenly Gnasher tensed. His ears shot forward and he half-rose to a crouch. His tail lashed, once, and every muscle was bunched as if to pounce.

Jon sat up. "What is it, Gnash? What have you seen?"

Gnasher answered with a very soft, low growl, as if he was warning Jon to be quiet. Suddenly it *was* quiet; there was a lull in the traffic, and for a few seconds all the smaller noises became audible. Jon's clock ticking. Wind rustling leaves in the garden. . .

And something else: a kind of *scritch-scritching* noise, like nothing Jon had ever heard before.

7

For one unnerving moment Jon thought the noise was in his room, and his stomach tightened unpleasantly. But then he realized that it wasn't *in* the house but outside. Almost directly below his window, in fact. He tried to remember what was down there. Only a patch of concrete, where the dustbins were. . .

Scritch-scritch. There it was again. Something scrabbling, quick and furtive, as if it were afraid of being caught. *Hey*, Jon thought, *it could be a fox! And I was only thinking about foxes a moment ago!*

Eagerly, he scrambled out of bed and went to the window. Gnasher didn't even glance at him; the cat was motionless now, and a peculiar gurgling noise came from his throat. The sky was clear and the moon high; with the street-lamp glow from the road beyond the disused railway cutting there was enough light to make out dim shapes in the garden.

Jon looked down towards the dustbins, and instantly the scrabbling stopped.

A train rattled and rumbled past on another stretch of track in the distance. As the sound faded Jon thought he heard a *click*, almost like a door closing, very close by. He craned forward, but couldn't quite see the dustbins.

Then something appeared. It moved so fast that it made him jump back from the window, and in the couple of seconds it took him to recover and look again, it was half-way across the garden.

It was keeping low to the ground, a darker blur in the darkness. It certainly wasn't a cat, and it wasn't a fox. Even Jon knew that foxes loped, like dogs. And this didn't lope; it *scuttled*, more like a rat than anything else.

Except for two things.

It wasn't the right shape for a rat. And rats didn't grow as big as German Shepherds.

2

Jon was still standing rigid with shock when suddenly Gnasher went crazy.

The cat shot upright, all four legs stiff, back arched and fur standing up along his spine. His tail, like a bottlebrush now, lashed madly from side to side. Then he uttered a howl that made Jon's own hair stand on end, and hurled himself at the glass pane.

"Gnash!" Jon grabbed at the cat, snatching him up, and spun back to the window.

The scuttling thing had vanished. Heart pounding, Jon stared out across the garden. He didn't believe anything that size could have moved so fast, but there was no trace of it. The garden was still and tranquil again.

"What *was* that?" His voice shook as he whispered the question aloud. He felt shocked and a bit sick, and when Gnasher wriggled out of his grip and dashed away, he hardly even noticed. He just kept staring . . . until at last common sense came to his rescue. Maybe it *had* been a fox or a cat, only the dark had distorted it so it looked far bigger than it really was. Or maybe it was only the shadow of a cloud passing across the moon. Or maybe he'd imagined the whole thing.

He swung round. Gnasher was sitting on the bed, his eyes looking like small, hot fires in the gloom. His tail was still bristling, but when Jon held out a hand to him he rubbed his head against it and purred. No, Jon told himself; he hadn't imagined it. Whatever it was, Gnasher had seen it too. But that didn't mean that it was some weird monster. Gnasher would attack anything, so the sensible answer was that he had seen just an ordinary animal, possibly even a mink. There were plenty of escaped minks in England, and they were quite big, weren't they?

He climbed back into bed, pushing Gnasher

over to make room. The cat settled down behind his knees, and he lay staring at the window and letting the traffic hum calm his nerves. He wondered if there would be any more scrabblings around the dustbins before morning.

There were no more scrabblings. If he had looked out an hour later, though, Jon might have seen the smaller, darker shapes that darted through the garden and away over the wall.

But by then, he was sound asleep.

Before breakfast the next morning, Jon investigated the garden.

There wasn't much to see. Most of it was grass, bald in some places and overgrown in others, and the flower-beds were full of dandelions. The wall at the end was only waist-high, and when Jon looked over at the railway cutting, he was disappointed. It was completely overgrown, a tangle of bushes and weeds and rubbish, with tall trees growing out of the mess. The rusting railway track lay at the bottom of the bank, and on the other side was a brick wall daubed with graffiti. Leaning over, Jon could just see what looked like a ruined station away to the left. It all looked decrepit; worth exploring, maybe, but, remembering last night, he wouldn't want to be an animal making its home in *that* lot!

But if Jon was disappointed by the garden, Gnasher loved it. He spent the morning staking out his territory. First he explored every inch of the ground. Then he intimidated the big tabby tomcat that lived three doors away. And by eleven o'clock he had brought home his first kill.

"Aargh! You *horrible* cat!" Gina shrieked when Gnasher carried his prey proudly into the flat. "Take it away, take it *out*!"

"It's only a mouse," said Jon.

"It's a *dead* mouse!"

"Oh." Jon peered. "Yeah. So it is. What's left of it."

"I don't want to know about that!" Gina was very squeamish. "Just get it out of my sight!"

Gnasher lost interest in the mouse and bounded back down to the garden, probably to catch another one. Jon wrapped the corpse in a piece of newspaper, and followed. Mum and Dad always put Gnasher's victims in the dustbin, but Jon didn't like that; it didn't seem right somehow. So instead, he found a trowel and went to give it a decent burial in the garden.

Here he met Frankie Lambert for the first time.

Jon was patting down earth over the buried mouse when a shadow fell across him and a voice said, "Hi. What are you doing?"

Frankie Lambert was several centimetres shorter than Jon, thin and wiry and with black hair and a sallow skin. He wasn't exactly a healthy outdoor type, but his smile was friendly enough. Jon introduced himself as the new neighbour.

"Hey, great!" Frankie said. "Mrs Walter – she lived there before you – was a real pain. Always telling me to keep quiet, don't do this, stop doing that – you know the kind of thing. I was really glad when she moved. What are your folks like?"

Jon said they were pretty OK, if you didn't count Gina, and which team did Frankie support? The name "Arsenal" cemented the friendship, and they spent the next hour kicking a ball around the garden while Jon asked what it was like living round here and what there was to do. It seemed this was an OK place. There was a park, a swimming-pool, some good burger bars and an open-air market. Lots to explore.

Then Frankie said, "What were you doing earlier? You looked like you were burying something."

Jon explained about Gnasher and the mouse. He felt a bit stupid, admitting that he'd bothered to bury it, but Frankie didn't seem to notice that. Instead, he frowned in the direction of a bush across the garden and said, "Oh. Just a mouse. . . You've got a cat, then?"

"Yeah. Big black-and-white one. He's called Gnasher. Why? Don't you like cats?"

Frankie hesitated a few moments before replying, "Oh . . . yes, I like them. But I'm a bit . . . allergic, that's all." He jerked his head with a nervous mannerism, and impatiently brushed something away from his face. "It's not just cats; dogs, too, and other things."

"Well, if Gnasher bothers you, just tell him to shove off," Jon reassured him. "He's not daft; he'll soon get the message."

As if conjured up by his words, Gnasher

appeared at that moment over the garden wall. He had obviously been in the cutting; there were leaves in his fur and cobwebs on his whiskers. Seeing Jon, he gave his usual greeting "Prrt!" and trotted towards him.

"Hi, Gnash!" Jon bent down to stroke the cat, then turned to Frankie. "Like I said, if he bothers you. . ."

He stopped. Frankie had backed away, and his face had an extraordinary expression. He looked wary, he looked guilty – and he looked *frightened*.

"Hey, it's OK." Jon straightened up. "He's really friendly; he loves people. Don't you, Gnash?"

He looked at the cat – and stopped again. Gnasher was staring – *glaring* – at Frankie. His head had dropped low to the ground, and his ears were flattened. Then, to Jon's astonishment, he hissed.

"Gnasher! What's the matter with you?" Jon reached out, but Gnasher dodged away, hissing again.

Frankie refused to meet Jon's baffled gaze. "Like I said, I'm a bit allergic," he mumbled. "Sorry."

Allergic? Jon thought. *Don't give me that!* Gnasher's reaction to Frankie wasn't about allergies, it was something else entirely. And the best word Jon could think of for it was hate.

Gnasher was growling now, a sort of *mwr-wr-wr-wr* sound. It wasn't his usual threat-growl, more of the *I-don't-like-this* that he usually reserved for a trip to the vet. Then suddenly he spat, turned tail and ran into the house.

"Sorry," Frankie said again.

Jon stared at the back door. "Well, at least he won't make a nuisance of himself." He looked sidelong, cannily, at Frankie. "With your allergy."

To his disappointment, Frankie didn't take the bait. He only shrugged and wandered off to the end of the garden. Following, and very curious, Jon tried to keep up the subject of cats.

"Gnasher must've been over in the cutting," he said. Reaching the wall, he peered over. "Brilliant place for a cat to explore. All those bushes. The line isn't used now, is it?"

"No." Frankie was staring at a brick in the wall.

"Good, then he won't get hit by a train. Have you ever been over there?"

"No," said Frankie sharply.

"Oh. Maybe we could, sometime. It might be a laugh."

Frankie said, "No!" yet again, but this time so ferociously that Jon looked at him in surprise.

"OK, there's no need to bite my head off!" He paused. "What's the problem, if the line isn't used any more?"

"Look, it's dangerous, all right?" Frankie had calmed down, though he still sounded edgy. "Even the dossers and winos won't go down there."

"Why not?"

A shrug. "There used to be a few of them round here; you'd see them in the streets in the daytime, and they slept in the station. Everyone knew about them. Then one disappeared, and a couple more vanished, too."

"What happened to them?"

Frankie looked evasive. "I wouldn't know. There was supposed to be some weirdo living rough in the old station building after the line was first closed. Then suddenly he wasn't there

18

any more. Some people reckon he died, but they never found a body. And there was this story about his ghost or something coming back."

"You don't believe that, do you?"

"Course I don't. But the dossers still disappeared, so word went out that it isn't a healthy place to hang around in." He lifted his head and, with an effort, looked Jon in the face. "Just don't go near it, Jon. Just *don't*."

It was then that Jon saw it: a look in Frankie's eyes, that he didn't quite have the skill to hide. Frankie was more than scared. He was *terrified*. And something desperate lurked behind his terror, as if he wanted very, very much to say more but didn't have the courage.

"Frankie—" Jon began.

Frankie interrupted before he could get any further. "I've got to go. My mum'll have lunch ready, and she kicks up if I'm late. See you! And remember what I said about the railway."

He turned on his heel and strode off towards the house. By the time he reached it he was running.

A couple of doors away, a dog had started barking angrily. Jon stared after Frankie, but didn't call out to him. Something was going on; he was as sure of it as he'd ever been of anything. And Frankie was involved. For just one moment it seemed he had been desperate to confide in Jon, but his nerve had failed.

All right, Jon thought. He'd give Frankie a bit of time. After all, they'd only just met each other; they weren't friends yet. A few days, maybe. Then if Frankie still wouldn't tell him what the mystery was, he'd have to find out for himself.

Whatever it took.

3

Making friends with Frankie Lambert wasn't the easiest job in the world. For one thing, Jon wasn't even sure that he *liked* his neighbour. He was wary and secretive and sometimes almost morose. They didn't have a lot in common. But that strange first encounter had aroused Jon's curiosity. There *was* something weird going on, and he was determined to get to the bottom of it.

With four weeks to go before the September term started, Jon had plenty of spare time. He asked Frankie to show him the area. Frankie couldn't refuse without seeming stand-offish, so the two of them spent hours mooching round the streets together. They didn't talk much. Once or twice Jon tried to steer Frankie on to the subject of the railway, but Frankie wouldn't be drawn.

Jon had started to notice a few other odd things about Frankie. To start with, he had some peculiar nervous mannerisms. He blinked a lot, as if the light was hurting his eyes. Sometimes his whole face twitched, too. When ever he seemed jumpy he'd keep brushing his mouth with the back of one hand, and when he realized he was doing it he would go red and look away.

They had a couple of football sessions in the park, and that was when Jon saw the Elastoplast. It was a big piece, on Frankie's left leg just below the knee, and the skin around it looked red and puffy.

"It's just a graze," Frankie said when Jon asked him. "It'll be OK in a couple of days."

But a couple of days later the Elastoplast was still there, and the puffy skin didn't look any better. In fact, Jon thought, it looked as if whatever was underneath was getting worse. And it was another thing that Frankie wouldn't talk about.

Then there were the animals.

Gnasher still hissed and growled whenever he saw Frankie – but, as Jon soon discovered, Gnasher was just the tip of the iceberg.

The first incident happened when the boys were walking down a side street, on their way home. A man with a dog on a lead appeared, coming towards them on the same side of the road, and Frankie stopped dead. Then, without any warning, he hurriedly crossed over.

"Frankie!" Jon checked for traffic then ran after him. "Where are you going?"

Frankie's face was white except for two spots of flaming pink on his cheeks. He mumbled something unintelligible, and Jon said, "Was it that guy? Do you know him, or something?"

"No," said Frankie and, hunching his shoulders, started off at a fast walk. Jon looked back across the road. The man was walking on – but the dog was straining sideways on its lead, staring, with its ears pricked aggressively.

Staring at Frankie.

Suddenly, the dog started to snarl. Then the snarls changed to a volley of barking that echoed the whole length of the street. The man shouted at it, jerking on the lead to make it behave.

And Frankie ran as fast as he could for home.

He wouldn't talk about it, of course. When Jon tried, he only said that it was his allergy and he'd always been scared of dogs anyway. Jon didn't believe a word. First, the dog was on a leash. Second, the fact that someone was allergic to an animal wouldn't make that animal snarl and threaten the way the dog – and Gnasher – had done.

Jon watched carefully after that, and his suspicions were soon confirmed. Animals *hated* Frankie. Cats avoided him, dogs barked at him in the street – even the birds in the garden were quiet whenever he was around. Frankie, in his turn, seemed as frightened of the animals as they were hostile to him, and he would go to almost any lengths to avoid meeting one.

And still Jon couldn't persuade Frankie to tell him what was going on.

On Friday morning, the boys were in the garden when Gnasher came over the wall from the railway cutting. For once he hadn't caught anything (he had brought home at least a dozen more mice or half-mice, to Gina's horror); he looked sidelong at Frankie, hissed as usual, and scurried indoors. As he vanished, Jon heard a rustling beyond the wall. He went to look over, and saw the neighbours' tabby tom slinking away through the undergrowth.

"All the cats love it down there," he observed. "Must be thousands of mice."

"Not just mice," said Frankie in a peculiar voice.

Jon turned. Frankie was standing a few paces away, his shoulders hunched and his eyes . . . well, *furtive* was the only way Jon could describe it.

Jon frowned. "What do you mean, not just mice?"

"Nothing." Frankie obviously wished he'd kept quiet, and turned his back. But Jon wasn't going to be put off this time.

"You must have meant something. What else is down there? Rats? Foxes? Mink? Pterodactyls?"

"Don't be stupid!"

"*Me*, stupid?" Jon retorted. "The way you go on, anyone'd think the place *had* got pterodactyls! They're probably nesting in the old station, so I'll get the fly-spray, shall I? Go down and give 'em a squirt. That stop you being so scared?"

"I'm not scared!"

"Oh, *sure* you're not! I mean, you don't *really* get antsy every time I say "station" or "railway", do you? I'm just imagining things!"

Suddenly Frankie squared up to Jon. His expression was angry, and for a second or two Jon really thought that he might swing a punch at him. But then the fury faded, and Frankie let out his breath in a hiss.

"Look," he said, "I've told you. Keep out of there." His face twitched and he brushed at his mouth. "If you've got any brain at all, just keep *out*!"

He spun round and walked off towards the house.

"Frankie!" Jon called.

"I'm going indoors." Frankie didn't look back, and a few moments later Jon heard the slam of the back door.

It was Frankie's attitude that made him do it. At least, that was what Jon told himself as he climbed over the wall; though he also had to admit that he'd been busting with curiosity ever since he first saw the abandoned cutting.

Well, his curiosity was going to get what it wanted. He hoped no one was looking out of a window; if Mum found out about this he'd be mincemeat. But no one yelled his name, so he swung his legs over the wall and, gingerly, let himself down.

It was a steep slope, but there were enough tree-roots sticking out of it to give plenty of foot- and hand-holds. Enough rubbish to start a landfill site as well, Jon thought as he began to slither carefully down. Rags, paper, rusty hub-caps, smashed-up bits of wood – you name it, all piled among the weeds and creepers. There was even what looked like a telegraph pole, with brambles twined stranglingly around it from end to end.

He could see the old station building more clearly now. Half its roof tiles had gone and by the look of it part of one wall had collapsed. But the platform was still there, and beyond that was the line itself. Everything was littered with rubbish, and there wasn't a living soul in sight. OK, Jon thought. So let's see what it is Frankie's so scared of.

His head was about two metres below the garden wall when he heard an inquiring "Prrt?" Looking up, he saw a furry face, two pointed ears, and amber eyes staring down eagerly.

Jon grinned. "Come on then, Gnash. Let's get the pterodactyls!"

Gnasher sprang over the wall and started down the slope, overtaking Jon and bounding sure-footedly to the bottom of the cutting. Jon followed, picking up bramble-scratches and jabs and a bruise or two, and scrambled the final few metres on to the station platform.

It was like standing in a long, dank, narrow valley. The cutting rose steeply to either side, blocking out the sunlight and turning everything murky. The railway line stretched away between the banks and under a rusty iron bridge before vanishing round a curve. There was a working railway track not far away – the old line had joined up with it once – but you'd never have known it now. The banks muffled sound, too. After the general background city noise it was eerily quiet. Nothing moved. The platform was bare, the station deserted. It looked and felt like a scene from a disaster movie, and Jon could easily have imagined that he was the only person left alive in the world.

Then something did move. It was Gnasher. He had dived into the old building, but now he emerged and wanted to start a game of chase. Jon joined in for a minute or two, running after him along the platform and pretending he didn't expect two ambushes, but then the cat lost interest and trotted back into the station again. Jon followed to look at the building more closely.

It really was in a state. Part of one wall *had* collapsed, and a section of the roof had come down with it, the beams lying criss-cross on the broken brickwork. All the door and windows had been boarded up, but the boards were rotten with damp and there was a man-sized hole at the ticket-office entrance.

Jon peered through the hole, hesitated, then stepped inside. The place was as gloomy as a tomb. It stank of mildew and worse, and it seemed unnaturally cold. Jon shivered. He could hear Gnasher clambering and scrabbling around somewhere in the depths of the building, but when he called, the cat took no notice.

Jon sighed. He ought not to go without Gnasher, but he didn't want to hang around any longer than he had to. The atmosphere down here was nasty, and he could understand why Frankie was so freaked.

Though Frankie claimed he had never come here. . .

Suddenly, Jon realized that he couldn't hear Gnasher any more. The scrabbling had stopped, and in its place was an ominous silence.

"Gnash?" Jon called uneasily.

No response.

"Gnasher! Where are you?"

Still nothing. Jon looked around. His pulse was beating uncomfortably fast, and it seemed to him that some of the shadows in the building were darker than they had been a few moments ago.

"Dumb cat. . ." Jon said it more for the comfort of hearing his own voice than for any other reason. He started to pick his way across the floor, climbing over rubble towards the fallen roof beams. Gnasher must be over there *somewhere*.

To his right, something scraped loudly.

Jon jumped as if he had been stung,

whipping round and staring into the dimness.

"Gnasher?" There was a quaver in his voice now, and his mouth was dry.

Then he heard something else. It took him a second or two to recognize it, but when he did, he felt as if all his blood had dried up and turned into dust.

It was the sound of something breathing.

Something large.

Something *very* large.

In the deep darkness of the station's inner rooms, a shadow moved, forming a crouching shape.

"What the. . ." The words died in Jon's throat. He could still hear the breathing. Then, piercing the air, came a high-pitched shriek.

And out of the dark, something launched itself towards him.

4

"*No-o-o!*" Jon staggered backwards, instinctively flinging up his arms to protect himself. His foot caught in a spar of wood – he felt himself falling but there was nothing he could do to stop it, and he crashed to the floor among a pile of debris. Panic exploded through his mind; he clasped both arms over his head, hunching, trying to make himself small.

"Mrrrwowr!"

The sound swamped Jon's terror like a deluge of ice-cold water. Slowly, very slowly, he sat up. . .

And saw Gnasher looking at him from where

he was balanced on a broken timber.

Gnasher, with a large and very dead rat dangling from his mouth.

Jon swore out loud. Of all the cretinous, pathetic *idiots*, he'd been scared out of his wits by nothing more than his own cat!

"*Mrrr! Mmmowr!*" Gnasher shook the rat as a terrier would. He looked enormously pleased with himself. Painfully, Jon climbed to his feet.

"You dumb animal!" he said grouchily. "Put it down!" Mum would go through the ceiling if Gnasher brought *that* indoors. But Gnasher didn't want to put the rat down, and when Jon tried to take it from him, he darted out of the door.

"*Gnasher!*" Jon went after the cat and was in time to see him scooting up the bank towards the garden wall. Shaking dust from his hair, he went wearily in pursuit. Climbing up was a lot harder than climbing down, and by the time he reached the top – after several sliding slips back – he was breathless and sweaty. Probably filthy too, but that couldn't be helped. Just have to hope that Mum had gone shopping or something.

To his relief, Gnasher hadn't taken the rat into the house. Instead, he was playing with it on the grass, batting the limp corpse around, throwing it up in the air and then pouncing on it. When Jon tried again to take it from him, he growled and ran off into the bushes, dragging his "toy" with him.

Jon was crawling on hands and knees under a lilac when Frankie came out and said, "Whatever are you doing?"

Jon wriggled backwards, wiping muddy hands. He opened his mouth, but before he could answer Frankie's question, Gnasher shot out from the bush, still with the rat, and started the batting-throwing-pouncing game again.

Frankie saw the rat. The colour drained from his face. Then he turned and ran into the house.

He came out again five minutes later. Gnasher was back in the bushes by this time, and Jon had given up trying to catch him. Frankie didn't say anything about the rat; he only asked if Jon wanted to go to the park that afternoon.

But he looked as if he had just been very sick indeed.

Gnasher finally lost interest in the rat. Jon

found it in a flower-bed when he and Frankie came back from the park, and he buried it where it lay, deep enough to stop the cat from being tempted to dig it up again.

The boys spent the evening in Frankie's room, watching videos. The rat wasn't mentioned, and Jon kept quiet about his expedition to the ruined station. Frankie was really twitchy tonight; that weird little mannerism was stronger than usual, and he couldn't keep his feet still. Fidget, shuffle, fidget – it got on Jon's nerves. Between the two movies Frankie went to the bathroom, and he was gone so long that Jon put his head outside to make sure everything was all right. The bathroom door was firmly shut, but he could hear a faint noise on the other side, like a *buzzing*. Baffled, Jon withdrew.

By the time Frankie came back, Jon's curiosity was boiling over. Saying, "Just going to the loo," he, too, went into the bathroom and, feeling a bit guilty but not *that* much, started to look around for clues.

He didn't find anything to explain the buzzing. But he *did* find the torn wrapper of a large Elastoplast in the waste bin.

* * *

In the middle of the night, Jon was woken by a rumbling noise.

It started in a dream, which (thanks to the videos) was about Samurai warriors invading a football ground. The dreaming Jon thought it was a giant earth-mover come to save the day, but even as he waited for it to roar into the stadium, he woke up.

The noise was still going on.

Jon shot upright in bed. Then, as he woke properly, he realized that the noise was much softer now, and didn't sound like an earth-mover after all. It was a very definite, and very familiar, growling.

Gnasher was on the windowsill. He had pushed his head and front paws between the curtains, so only his back half showed. His tail was lashing, and his body quivered with angry excitement.

"Gnash?" Jon climbed out of bed. "What is it? What have you seen?"

He recalled the strange shadows in the garden a few nights ago, and had a sudden attack of nerves as he cautiously lifted back the curtain. Tonight, though, the sky was cloudy, and without the moon, the distant street lamps didn't give enough light to make out much of the garden. All Jon could see was inky darkness with a few vague, even darker patches where the bushes were. But Gnasher's night vision was far better. And from the way the cat was acting, Jon knew there was something out there.

He narrowed his eyes, peering harder. No use; he still couldn't distinguish anything.

Unless. . .

One of the dark patches was near the garden wall. It couldn't be a bush, because it was in the middle of the grass. And it was . . . *moving*, wasn't it? Moving slowly, furtively. As if it were searching for something. . .

Jon licked dry lips. Maybe if he opened the window . . . he'd have to hold Gnasher back, but without the glass in the way, he might be able to see a bit better.

Grasping the cat firmly with one hand, he reached with the other for the window catch.

The catch squeaked. It was only a small noise, but that was enough. The unknown thing on the lawn heard it and moved, fast. Jon had one glimpse of the dark patch scurrying across the grass, then it flowed over the wall and disappeared.

"*Rwwww. . .*" said Gnasher crossly, and his tail lashed again before he wriggled free from Jon's grip, jumped down and went to sulk under the bed.

Jon let out a slow breath. That thing could certainly shift when it wanted to! He still had no idea what it was – but at least he knew, now, where it came from.

Its lair must be somewhere in the cutting.

In the morning, Gnasher's rat had gone.

Jon found the hole and the scrabbled earth when he went outside before breakfast. *Something* had come in the night, dug up the corpse and made off with it. The obvious culprit was a dog – but Jon knew better. He had glimpsed the intruder with his own eyes, and no dog had ever moved like that.

He didn't say a word to anyone about the incident. He simply put the disturbed earth back, and thought his own thoughts, which were very far from restful.

That morning, Gnasher started on a rat-catching spree at the derelict station. Time and again Jon saw him slinking over the garden wall, and time and again he was back within half an hour, proudly carrying another victim. By the end of the day he had brought back eight. Jon buried them all, but then decided that enough was enough. He was beginning to feel like a full-time gravedigger – any more, and they could go straight in the dustbin!

At least, he thought, Gnasher had the decency to kill his prey before he brought it home. He could just imagine the fireworks if live rats escaped and got into the house – Mum and Dad would have fits and Gina would probably die of a heart attack.

And as for Frankie. . .

He didn't know whether Frankie saw Gnasher bringing any of the rats home. Frankie was "busy" today; a school holiday project, he said. Jon accepted the explanation, though privately he didn't believe it. Frankie had been in a filthy mood when they met briefly in the morning. He'd snapped Jon's head off twice, then mumbled an apology and, brushing at his mouth, hurried indoors. He had some marks on his arms, Jon noticed; red and angry, almost like a rash. And Frankie kept scratching his left leg where the Elastoplast had been – or still was.

Jon meant to keep watch that night, in case the mysterious creature returned to the garden. But in the end he couldn't stay awake, and he slept until Dad woke him in the morning.

The rats he'd buried in the garden had gone. More holes, more thrown earth, no bodies. So it had come back. But why? What could any animal possibly want with *eight* dead rats? Was it eating them – or was it taking them back to its unknown hideaway, maybe to feed its young?

The thought that there might be a whole nest of the mysterious creatures made Jon very uneasy indeed. He wondered if he should go to the old station again and have a *really* good look around. But the idea didn't appeal; at least, not on his own. And there wasn't anyone he could ask to come with him.

Gnasher continued cheerfully with Operation Anti-Rat. His tally on the second day was only five, all of which went in the dustbin and none of which (to Jon's relief) Mum saw. The dustmen came early in the morning, before Jon had time to check whether the corpses were still there, but if there were any midnight disturbances, he slept through them.

The third night, though, was different.

Gnasher's total that day was six. Lucky the dustmen had been, or the bin would have been overflowing with bodies, Jon thought. He ought to get a board and start notching up Gnasher's kills, like a wartime fighter pilot.

Tired out by his efforts, Gnasher slept on the best chair for most of the evening. But at two a.m. he was back on Jon's windowsill, and growling loudly enough to wake him.

Jon sat up in bed, suddenly and sharply alert. There was a noise outside, right below his window. Faint, but he'd heard it distinctly. A rattle, then a slight, cautious scraping. . .

He was out of bed and across the floor in a second. Gnasher made an eager "*Wowwrr!*" sound, and gingerly Jon drew back the curtain.

The dustbins were just out of sight under the back porch – but if he couldn't quite see them, Jon *could* see the shadow that moved near them. It was hunched over, busy with some-thing. There was another faint rattle, and suddenly Jon knew what the noise was.

Someone – or something – was very carefully

taking one of the dustbin lids off.

No dog or fox or mink could do that, Jon thought. *So what was down there?* He didn't move; he didn't even breathe. Even Gnasher was motionless, as if he knew how important it was not to attract attention. For a few seconds there was no noise at all. Then came the muffled *thud* of the dustbin lid being put back, and a moment later the shadow was scuttling away across the grass.

The sky was only patchily cloudy tonight, and abruptly the moon came out, brightening the garden. Suddenly Jon could see the running shape more clearly – and see, too, the smaller shadows that waited for it at the garden's far end. There must have been ten or twelve of them. They started to move as the big shadow reached them, and like a small, dark tide they all scrambled over the wall and vanished into the cutting.

Jon stood rigid, hands pressed to the window, eyes and mouth wide open. He was too stunned to move, but his mind was whirling as the truth crashed into his brain.

He knew, now, what the large shadow was. Just for one moment he had seen and recognized its true shape. It wasn't an animal; it was human.

And he was certain it was Frankie.

5

The following day, Jon buried Gnasher's tally of rats in the flower-bed.

There were five again, and he took good care to dig the holes for them a good distance apart from each other. If the intruder came to retrieve them tonight – and Jon was convinced it would – then it would have to spend a while at the task, long enough for Jon to act.

The intruder. Rationally, he couldn't believe that the hunched, shadowy figure scurrying through the garden last night could possibly have been Frankie. He had *thought* he recognized him – his shape, his hair – but the idea was so crazy that he told himself he must have been mistaken.

Yet if it wasn't Frankie, who was it? For Jon was certain of one thing. The intruder *was* human.

So tonight he was determined to find out the truth once and for all.

He spent most of the evening in his room, making two lists: one of the facts he knew, the other of the things he could only guess at. The result was horribly confusing. The trouble was, Jon told himself, he didn't really *know* much at all, and the few clues he had made no sense. Even the weird things about Frankie didn't add up to anything solid; and as for his gut feeling that there was a connection with the abandoned railway . . . well, that was pure hunch.

He went to bed early, making sure that Gnasher was in his room. If he fell asleep and anything happened, the cat would start growling again and wake him. However, tonight he was too keyed-up – and probably too nervous – to sleep. Shortly after midnight the noise of the TV stopped, then there were footsteps along the landing and the hall light went out. Jon lay in the dark, listening until he was sure everyone else was asleep, then he got out of bed and went to sit at the window with Gnasher.

There were no clouds tonight and the moon was nearly full, so Jon could see the garden pretty well. For a while he watched tree-shadows making patterns on the grass, but soon he became bored and sleepy. *Watch it!* he thought. *You've got to stay awake!* He went to his desk, switched his computer on and found a game that didn't need sound. He was engrossed in it, and building up a high score, when suddenly Gnasher snarled.

Jon jumped, and looked towards the window. Gnasher was up on his hind legs, just as he had been before, staring fixedly out. Forgetting the game, Jon ran to join him.

And saw Frankie in the garden.

It *was* Frankie! In the bright moonlight there could be no doubt of it. He was creeping stealthily towards the flower-bed, and he had a trowel in his hand. Reaching the spot where the first rat was buried, he started to dig quickly in the loosened earth, and in less than a minute he had retrieved the corpse. Then on to the next, and the next. *He must have watched me*, Jon thought. *He must have seen exactly where I buried every one!*

Frankie unearthed the last rat, and straightened up. Holding his prizes by their tails, he looked quickly around, then headed for the garden wall. Reaching it, he scrambled over, dropped down and disappeared on the far side.

Jon was still fully dressed, and in seconds he was out on the landing. Gnasher tried to follow, but Jon couldn't have him giving the game away, and shut the bedroom door in his indignant face. Key, key – yes, it was in his pocket. He let himself out of the flat and hurried as quickly and quietly as he could down the stairs to the ground floor.

The back door stood open. In the strong moonlight the garden looked unearthly, and Jon's skin prickled nervously as he stepped outside. Everything was black and silver, no colour anywhere. He felt as if something was watching him.

Oh, shut up! he told his imagination. Frankie had gone and there was nothing else out here. What was there to be scared of?

He took a deep breath and set off.

The garden was very different at night. The

friendly, familiar atmosphere of daytime had completely vanished, replaced by an eerie, breathless feeling, as if the world was waiting for something unpleasant. There was still the traffic hum, and a long, slow goods train was rattling along a track in the far distance; but somehow they sounded unreal, as if they belonged to another world.

The trees were rustling. Jon could hear them as he approached the wall – a dry, secretive whispering. The nervous prickling was getting worse, and the house, when he glanced uneasily back at it, seemed nearly as remote as the traffic and train. Maybe he shouldn't have come out here. He'd never find Frankie. Maybe he should just go back indoors, go to bed and forget this whole stupid idea.

Then, beyond the wall, he heard the crunch of bushes and the snap of a breaking twig.

Frankie! It had to be! Curiosity overcame everything else and, running the last few paces to the wall, Jon leaned over and looked into the cutting.

Frankie was there. Despite the trees' shadows Jon could see him clambering through the tangle of greenery and rubbish, heading down towards the ruined station.

For some unimaginable reason, Frankie was taking the rats Gnasher had killed down to the old station. Taking them back to where they had lived? It was possible. But whatever *for*?

Frankie had almost reached the platform. In another minute he would be out of sight. Jon had a wild urge to follow him and see what happened, but it faded quickly. He had only made that climb once; to try to do it in the dark would be insane. No, he had seen all he could for the time being.

Tomorrow, though, would be another matter.

He took a last look at Frankie, while a hundred questions seethed in his mind. Then he turned and hurried back into the house.

Frankie came back an hour later.

Jon saw him from his window. Sleep was right out of the question, so he had waited and watched. When the slight figure appeared over the wall, he drew back out of sight, but Frankie didn't even think of looking up. He moved slowly, dragging his feet. He looked desperately tired. Half-way to the house he stopped and rubbed one hand over his face, as if he was trying to wipe something away. Then he scratched his leg – the one with the plaster on it – before starting wearily forward again. Moments later Jon heard the soft sound of the back door closing, and then there was silence.

He let the curtain fall and sat down on his bed. Even allowing for the time it took him to climb down and back, Frankie must have been at the old station for a good half hour. What had he been *doing*?

Then Jon remembered what Frankie had told him when he first warned him away from the station. Some weirdo who used to live rough there. And he had died. And there were tales about his ghost coming back to haunt the place.

So had Frankie made that story up, to scare him off? Was the ghost stuff a cover for something else, that he didn't want anyone else to find out about?

Well, if Frankie thought he had succeeded in putting Jon off the scent, he was wrong. The ruined station was the key to this mystery. And keys opened doors. The vital clue must be somewhere in or near that building, and Jon was determined to find it.

When he did, Frankie Lambert would have some questions to answer!

6

Next morning, Jon went downstairs to see Frankie.

He had no intention of saying anything about what had happened last night, but he wanted to see if anything about Frankie had changed. And he still couldn't shake off the feeling that, deep down, Frankie was desperate to talk. So at least he could give him the chance, and if he wouldn't take it, well, that was his bad luck.

Frankie's mum answered the door. Hoping he sounded casual, Jon said, "Hello, Mrs Lambert. Is Frankie in?"

"Well, yes," said Frankie's mum, "but we're going out soon." She called over her shoulder, "Fran-*kie*! Jon's here!"

Frankie appeared. He didn't ask Jon in but came out to the hall, pulling the door to behind him.

"You going somewhere?" Jon asked.

Frankie nodded gloomily. "My gran's coming up from Kent and we're meeting her in the West End." He pulled a face. "Shopping. I can't get out of it; I'm supposed to choose my birthday present."

"Oh. When's your birthday, then?"

"Next month. Knowing Gran, I'll get a choice between Lego and a Thomas the Tank Engine duvet. She still thinks I'm about four."

"Oh," Jon said again, privately hardly able to believe his good luck. "Pity. I thought you might fancy a kick around the park."

"I would've. Tomorrow, maybe?"

"Yeah, why not? I'll go up there anyway. Better than hanging around here on my own." And better than letting Frankie suspect anything about him and the station, Jon thought. He backed towards the stairs. "See you, then. Happy shopping!"

"Thanks a bunch," said Frankie, and slammed the door.

Jon waited until he saw the Lamberts leave, then he went out to the garden and climbed over the wall.

Getting down was easier the second time. He'd found out the hard way where some of the pitfalls – and the worst of the brambles – were, and he reached the derelict platform without too many battle-scars.

The station didn't look any different. Not that there was any logical reason why it should have done, but after last night Jon had wondered if anything might have changed. He started by searching around outside the building, looking for signs of what Frankie might have been doing last night. There was nothing. Well, he asked himself, what had he expected to find? Rat-sized graves with little carved headstones? Letters burned into the brick wall – THE GHOST LIVES HERE? Or maybe a flashing neon sign with arrows, saying, HI, JON, THIS WAY TO THE MYSTERY? There wasn't even a telltale footprint; in this weather the ground was too dry.

He heard a rustle in the undergrowth behind him and whipped round. No sign of anything . . . but a bush about a quarter of the way up the bank was quivering as if something small and fast had disturbed it. Probably a rat, Jon thought grimly. He should have brought Gnasher, not left him snoring peacefully on his bed. . .

Oh, stop being dumb! He didn't need a cat to protect him! Anyway, Gnasher would just have made a nuisance of himself, poking his nose in everywhere and giving the game away.

Away to who? said a small, inner voice. Jon shivered, and told himself not to be so feeble. Flat fact: there wasn't anyone else here, only rats, mice, spiders, cockroaches and whatever other wildlife you'd expect to infest a place like this. Stop dithering around, and get on with it!

He had brought a torch this time, and as he squeezed through the splintered boards over the station door, he fished it from his pocket and switched it on. It didn't seem to make a lot of difference. The place still looked as gloomy as Dracula's castle, and all the torch beam did was show up the cobwebs that festooned everything like curtains. Turning slowly in a full circle, Jon tried to get his bearings. This must have been the ticket office, and through there, where part of the roof had come down, would be the waiting room and then the ladies' and gents' loos. Maybe there would have been another office, too, for the station-master or whoever. OK, the ticket office looked just the same as when he last saw it. So how about investigating a bit further?

He shone his torch through the triangular gap where the roof beam had crashed down. Couldn't see much in there, except for rubble and more timbers. If he wanted a clearer look, he would have to go in.

Something creaked ominously overhead when he started to ease through the gap. Jon paused, looking up nervously, but there was no sign of anything else collapsing. Anyway, he told himself, there wasn't much more of that section left to fall down; it was nearly all hole and no roof. Another wriggle and he was clear, stumbling over chunks of plaster and broken bricks and nearly losing his balance as he had done on the first visit. Righting himself, he swept the torch-beam around. This room was bigger than the first, and in far more of a mess.

There was rubbish everywhere, even some smashed-up furniture by the look of it. If he wanted to get across to the other side, he'd have to shift this bit of. . .

The thought died in Jon's mind as, from the innermost depths of the building, he heard something shuffle.

He froze, and the noise stopped too. An echo? No, couldn't be: it wasn't the least like any sound he had made. Slowly, and very cautiously, Jon began to shine his torch around again.

As the beam fell on the darkest corner of the room, a shadow moved quickly and there was a *swish-scrabble-swish*, as though something bulky was ducking out of sight.

Sensations of blazing heat and icy cold chased each other over Jon's skin, and the torch beam wavered as his hand started to shake. There was something alive in that corner – and it was big!

No, wait! he told himself. *Get a grip!* It was a rat. Had to be. Just a rat, scurrying into hiding as the torchlight caught it, and in this enclosed space the noise sounded much louder than it really was.

Then, suddenly, it came again – the scrabbling, further away now. It sounded as if it was below floor level. The station must have a cellar – but even as that thought entered Jon's mind, it was swamped by a horrible realization.

He could hear something else. Rhythmic, regular, a muffled, husky noise that rose and fell and rose and fell.

Breathing.

And it wasn't the breathing of any rat Jon had ever imagined, let alone seen.

He took a pace backwards. Instantly the breathing stopped, as though whatever – or whoever – was there had sensed him moving and was keeping very, very still. In one way that was reassuring, suggesting it was more afraid of him than he was of it.

Unless the stillness meant that it was getting ready to pounce. . .

With an enormous effort, Jon dragged his shuddering nerves under control. Ghosts, monsters, predators – he was thinking like a little kid, terrified of his own shadow! If the breathing had been too loud to be a rat, then it was something bigger but just as ordinary. Fox. Dog. Even a human being. Maybe Frankie had been wrong about the dossers.

OK, Jon, you came down here to find

something out, didn't you? he asked himself fiercely. *So get on with it. Starting with this.*

He wetted his lips with his tongue and called out, softly,

"Hello? Who's there?"

Shuffle-swish! A puff of dust billowed up into the torchlight, and something shifted beyond the beam's range. If it was a dosser, he was scared all right. And he must have got himself right in beyond the next section of wall. The roof was nearly intact there, making it much darker than anywhere else in the building – the ideal sort of place for someone to shelter or hide. If Jon wanted to see anything, he would have to climb through.

He started forward, slowly and carefully, through a ragged gap where an inside door must once have been. It was dark as pitch now, and there was an awful smell that he couldn't recognize.

Then the breathing started again.

It *was* coming from below. There was a cellar, then. But where was the entrance? Ranging the torch from side to side, Jon suddenly paused as the light showed up a larger than usual pile of rubble, with a mound of earth beside it.

Someone had been digging. Questions boiled up in Jon's mind and he scrambled towards the spot. As he got closer, the torch showed a hole in the floor. It was more than a metre across, and the floorboards around it weren't merely splintered but smashed. The hole looked deep, though he wasn't at the right angle yet to see to the bottom. And the horrible smell was much stronger.

"What on earth. . .?" Jon whispered the words aloud without realizing it.

And was answered by a soft squeak.

He spun round. Behind him, on the floor, were six very large rats. They were sitting up on their haunches, front paws raised, staring at him.

Then he saw eight more in the doorway. These were smaller – more like normal size – but they were sitting up, too. Very still. Very quiet. *Staring*.

Jon swallowed. He moved the torch – and there were more rats, on a fallen beam that lay at a sloping angle between the ceiling and the floor. Lined in a row, sitting up, and absolutely motionless as they watched with their mean, beady little eyes.

The ugly truth dawned on Jon even before

he started to swing the torch around in a wide arc. There were rats everywhere. Dozens and dozens of them, perched on the rubble, squatting on the broken timbers, lurking in every cranny. Not a muscle twitched and not a whisker moved. But the cold gaze of each and every rat was fixed unwaveringly on his face.

Jon started to feel sick. He wasn't squeamish about rats; in the ordinary way he wasn't scared of them at all. This, though, was different. There was something horribly *knowing* about the way these rats were looking at him. It was almost as if they had one single mind.

Or as if something far, far more intelligent was controlling them. . .

He took an unsteady step backwards. As one, the rats on the floor moved as well, keeping precisely the same distance between themselves and him. Another step, another quick movement. And now the ones on the fallen beam were closing in. They didn't take their eyes off him for an instant. Suddenly, unpleasantly, Jon realized that by backing away from them, he was getting nearer to the hole in the floor.

Which was, perhaps, exactly what they wanted him to do.

Don't panic! Jon's floundering brain told him. The rats were trying to drive him towards the hole, but he didn't have to obey. However many of them there were, he was far bigger and stronger. All he had to do was step over them – jump over them, if necessary – and run for the door. They couldn't stop him. They *couldn't*.

He drew a huge breath, and lunged forward.

Everything happened so fast then that it was blurring chaos in Jon's mind. A shrill, racketing noise echoed through the room – it was the rats squealing, though he didn't know it then – and from behind him came a slither and a *whoosh*. An enormous shadow flicked across his wildly swinging torch beam, and something big and dark barrelled at him from behind. Jon yelled in terror, flailing for the door – then a ferocious hiss cut through the mayhem, and a small black-and-white shape streaked from outside and across the floor.

Gnasher! Snarling, the cat launched himself at the oncoming darkness. Jon heard a piercing squeal and Gnasher's furious yowl as he attacked, and horror hit him. *Gnasher was too small to hurt that thing – he'd be killed!*

Despite his own terror Jon turned instinctively to grab for Gnasher and drag him out. As he did so, something cannoned into him. The torch flew from his grasp and went spinning, hitting the floor, and the bulb shattered, bringing darkness crashing down. Jon yelled again, kicking out. His foot connected. There was an enraged grunt, a scuffling in the murky gloom – and a searing pain shot through Jon's right arm as something bit him before whipping round and darting away, hurling up a cloud of choking dust.

Jon never remembered how he got out of the station building. All he knew was that suddenly he was on the platform, gasping, blinking in the daylight, with Gnasher in his arms. The cat struggled furiously; he wanted to get back in there. But Jon held on to him; held on, too, to the sickness that was threatening to surge from his stomach and make him throw up.

And ran.

7

His arm *hurt*. It hadn't bled much, but it was throbbing hotly, and when Jon had the chance to look at it properly he didn't like what he saw. The skin around the bite was very red, and in the middle of the redness was a pattern of small puncture wounds. Teeth marks.

But what sort of teeth?

Still clutching the protesting Gnasher, Jon had half-scrambled and half-fallen over the garden wall and kept on running until he was inside the house. Mum was out. That was an enormous relief, for he would have had a hard time explaining this. ("What's happened to your arm, Jon?" "Oh, nothing, Mum, I was just messing around in the old station when something bit me.") Mum would have gone ballistic. Luckily, the bite was on Jon's upper arm, far enough above the elbow to be easily hidden. He would wash and disinfect it, then put a plaster on. It wasn't anything serious.

He was still shaking as he cleaned the bite. When it was nearly done, his stomach heaved and this time he did throw up. Gnasher was pacing up and down by the flat door, lashing his tail and growling, but Jon felt too rough to take any notice of him. All he wanted was to go to sleep – shock, he supposed. Certainly he didn't want to think about what had just happened. Not yet.

But over the next few days he had to think about it, and think hard. Because things were starting to happen to him that he neither understood nor liked.

To begin with, the bite wasn't healing properly. It didn't seem to be infected, but the surrounding skin was still red and the teeth-marks weren't fading. Jon had some other weird symptoms, too. In the mornings his whole body itched and prickled. The feeling went away after a while but then came back at odd moments throughout the day, more and more often as time went by. He knew he should have told Mum about it, but he didn't dare. Mum would hustle him straight off to the doctor, and then there would be awkward questions to answer – he couldn't face that. The symptoms would go soon. Surely they would?

But they didn't. Instead, they got worse. And other strange things were starting to happen. Jon's face developed a twitch that he couldn't control, and with it a sensation in his nose like the excruciating tickle just before a sneeze. He was also finding his temper very hard to control – he kept getting flashes of vicious anger, not directed at anyone in particular but just *there*. It reached the stage where he was half scared to be with anyone, in case he blew up at them like a volcano for no good reason. Even Gnasher seemed to be avoiding him.

Then there were the dreams. Jon couldn't remember ever having had such diabolical nightmares in his life. They were like every horror movie he had ever seen rolled into one, and so real that he woke from them whimpering and sweating. Every night it was the same.

He never recalled the details once he was awake, but before long he was afraid to go to sleep, because he knew that the dreams would come to haunt him again.

The one small consolation he had was that Gnasher had stopped catching rats. Jon didn't want to see another rat again as long as he lived. For that matter, it didn't bother him if he didn't see anything of Gnasher, either. He was *glad* that the cat didn't come near him. He didn't want him around. In fact, he realized angrily, he didn't want anyone around at all. And especially not Frankie Lambert.

He hadn't seen Frankie since the day he was bitten. Frankie hadn't appeared in the garden, hadn't called at the flat, and Jon had no intention of going to see him. In fact, he thought as he mooched into the kitchen one morning, this was all Frankie's fault. If it hadn't been for his stupid secrecy about the old station, Jon would never have climbed down there, and never have been attacked. One day, he told himself savagely, he would get even with Frankie. He'd wait until there was no one around, and then he'd—

His growing fury erupted suddenly in a surge

of blind rage, and he snatched up a coffee mug and hurled it at the wall. It shattered in an explosion of china fragments, and as Jon, stunned, stared at the mess, Mum came hurrying in.

"Jon? What's going on?" Then she saw the broken shards. "Oh! That was my favourite. What happened?"

"Nothing," Jon said through clenched teeth.

Mum paused, looking keenly at him. "Your face is flushed. Are you all right?"

"*Yes!*" Jon snapped. "Just leave me alone, will you?"

"Well, thank you very much!" said Mum huffily. "You break my favourite mug and you can't even say sorry; you just bite my head off! Honestly, Jon, I don't know what's the matter with you lately. You're so ratty!"

Stupidly, cretinously, it had never occurred to Jon before – but as Mum said the word, the bombshell dropped in his mind.

Ratty.

She didn't know how right she was.

"Jon!" Mum shouted after him as he turned and ran out of the kitchen. Jon ignored her. He rushed into the bathroom, slammed and locked the door, and pressed his forehead against the cold glass of the mirror until his banging heart slowed down.

Idiot, idiot, *idiot*! The truth had been right in front of him all along, and he hadn't *seen* it. He was ratty, all right! The twitching, the itching, the filthy moods and bursts of animal fury – he was behaving, and feeling, exactly like a rat.

Exactly like Frankie.

Jon raised his head and stared at himself in the mirror. For a moment he was terrified that his face would have changed and he'd see fur, a sharp nose and beady little eyes looking back at him. The relief when his own normal self looked back at him was overwhelming.

But it didn't change the facts: the wound that wouldn't heal. Exactly like Frankie. The twitching. Exactly like Frankie. Was he, too, starting to brush at his mouth with his hands, as Frankie did? He hadn't caught himself doing it yet, but the gesture was just like a rat brushing at its whiskers with its paws.

Suddenly, Jon badly needed some fresh air. He shoved the window as wide open as it would go, and leaned out. The bathroom was at the front of the house, overlooking the street, and as he looked down to the pavement Jon saw two women walking by underneath. One of them had a small terrier on a lead; the dog looked up, spotted him. . .

And started to bark furiously.

Jon dodged back inside and shut the window. All right, he told himself; all *right*! It might just be a coincidence. Maybe the terrier was one of those dogs that barked at anything.

But he didn't think so. Something was happening to him that he couldn't control and couldn't begin to understand. Something that no one would believe.

Except for Frankie. Because it was happening to him, too. And Jon was convinced that Frankie knew the whole truth about the station and what lurked down there in the ruined building.

He jumped as a knock sounded on the bathroom door and Mum's voice called, "Jon? Are you all right?"

Jon swallowed, and drew breath. "Yes," he called back. "I'm OK." He had to put Mum off the scent; his anger was completely gone now, and taking a grip on himself he unlocked the door and opened it.

"Sorry, Mum," he said quietly.

"It doesn't matter, love." Mum sounded concerned. "Look . . . is anything wrong? Anything you want to talk about?"

He shook his head. "No. It isn't anything, honestly. I was just being . . . ratty, like you said. I won't do it again. Promise."

On impulse, he hugged her. It was a long time since he had done that, and Mum was astonished and pleased.

"Well," she said uncertainly, "if you're sure—"

"Course I am. Look, I – I think I'll go downstairs. See if Frankie's around."

"All right. That sounds like a good idea. See you later, then."

Gnasher was at the end of the hall. He saw Jon, hissed, and ran into the sitting room. Mum didn't notice. She watched as Jon went out of the flat, but she didn't say any more.

Frankie answered Jon's knock. He blinked, as if taken aback, then said, "Oh – hi. How's things?"

Jon didn't answer the question. "You busy?" he said.

71

A pause. Frankie had his sweatshirt sleeves pushed up, Jon noticed, and his arms had that funny red rash again. Then Frankie shrugged.

"Not specially, I suppose. I've still got this project to finish, but—"

"Oh, yeah," Jon interrupted. "The project. Your favourite excuse."

Frankie's eyes narrowed. "What do you mean?"

"I mean, your favourite excuse for avoiding me. I want to talk to you, Frankie." Jon could feel the animal anger starting to rise up in him again. Fighting it with all his strength, he went on more calmly, "Look, it's important. Are your folks in?"

"No-o . . . but. . ."

"Good." Frankie wasn't strong enough to stop Jon as he pushed past him and into the flat. "Because I don't want anyone else to hear what I've got to say, and I don't suppose you do either."

Now Frankie was looking very evasive. "Can't tell until I know what it is, can I?"

"Right." Jon stopped in the hall. From here he could see into three rooms: the sitting room, Frankie's bedroom and the bathroom.

Nothing interesting in the sitting room. The bedroom was a tip, as usual. The bathroom. . .

A battery razor was lying on a shelf near the basin.

And the basin had hair scattered all over it.

Or rather, *fur*.

Frankie saw Jon looking, and drew breath in a quick, sharp gasp. Jon didn't say a word. He just pushed up his right sleeve, held his arm out, then with a jerk pulled off the plaster, exposing the bite-mark.

"How's yours?" he said challengingly.

Frankie's face turned white. "*When did—*" He snapped the words off.

"The day you had to meet your gran," Jon told him. "Do you want to know why I went down there? I'll tell you. Because the night before, I saw you in the garden. I saw you dig those dead rats up, and I saw you go over the wall and down the cutting. What's going on, Frankie? I want to know, *right now!*"

Frankie hesitated for perhaps half a second, then swung away. "I don't know what you're talking about."

"Oh, yes you do!" Jon shouted. "Come on, Frankie – stop messing me around, and tell the truth! It bit you, didn't it? Whatever that thing is down there, it bit you, and—"

"*No!*" Frankie yelled. He was nearly in tears. "Shut up! Just shut up and go away and leave me *alone!*"

There was silence. Jon could see Frankie's shoulders shaking, and suddenly he felt disgusted. It wasn't worth trying to make him see reason. There was only one thing he could do.

"All right," he said contemptuously. "If you're too much of a coward to tell me what's going on, I'll just have to find out for myself, won't I?"

Frankie turned round as Jon started to walk out of the flat. "Where are you going?"

"Back to the station. To see what really *is* down there."

Frankie grabbed at his arm. "You mustn't!"

Jon shook him off, glaring. "You know how to stop me," he challenged. "Tell the truth!"

Frankie's face was frozen and miserable. He didn't answer.

"Thought not," Jon said, and strode out.

"Jon, *please*—"

The door slammed in Frankie's face.

8

If Jon had been thinking calmly, if he'd had any sense at all, he wouldn't have gone near the old station again at any price. But the sensible part of him was buried under an avalanche of blind, animal anger – anger not just at Frankie, but at the whole world. That was how it felt, anyway, as he scrambled down the last steep slope of the cutting and on to the platform.

He headed straight for the station building. He didn't even have a torch this time, which really was about as stupid as it was possible to get. But, again, the rational part of his mind simply wasn't working.

One of the rotting boards over the door had shifted, blocking the gap. Jon thumped and kicked at it until it splintered, taking his rage out on it. It made him feel better. Then he was inside the station.

The stench he'd noticed before was much stronger – either that or his sense of smell was more acute, which, he thought grimly, was pretty likely. It didn't seem quite so dark in here, either. It was as if his eyesight, too, was sharper, more like an animal's. . .

There were no rats around this time. In fact everything seemed unnaturally quiet and still. A small voice at the back of Jon's brain woke up and whispered to him, *Maybe they're waiting for something.* But he thrust it away. He wasn't frightened. He should have been, but he wasn't.

Not yet, anyway. . .

He picked his way across the rubble to the far side of the ticket office. The big, fallen roof beam looked as if it had moved, and Jon examined it more closely. Yes, the angle of it had changed, and there was a scraped line in the dust on the floor, where the beam's end had slid along. Was the building subsiding?

Or had something else done this?

Over there was the door that led to the innermost, and darkest, part of the building. Jon stared speculatively at it, remembering what had happened in there before, and for a moment his nerve almost failed. *This was mad! He shouldn't be here; he should have—*

The thought snapped off as the anger took hold again, and with it a sort of ugly bravado that wasn't like any human feeling. It said, *I want,* and *I will*, and it carried Jon with it, so that almost before he knew what he was doing he had crossed the room and shoved through into the heart of the station.

Here it was hard to see clearly. He could make out the shapes of things among the shadows, but that was about all. The smell was overpowering but it didn't revolt him. In fact he almost *liked* it. It was familiar. Comforting. A smell of . . . *home.* Jon's face twitched and he rubbed his mouth with one hand without realizing it. *Over there*, said an instinct somewhere deep inside him. *Over there, where the floorboards are smashed and the earth's piled up. That's where I want to go. That's where I've **got** to go.*

It wasn't a cellar, it was just a hole – a ragged-shaped patch like spilled oil beside the heap of dug-out earth. It didn't go straight down but sloped away at an angle, like a tunnel leading away under the station. There were strange ribbed marks in the dust around its edges, arcs and half-circles, as if someone had swished a broom across the surface.

A broom? Jon asked himself. *Or a huge tail?*

Somewhere within him, reason was was screaming and yelling at him: *Don't do this! Don't be so insane! Just get out of this evil place!* Jon didn't listen. He couldn't listen. All he heard was the other voice that told him he had to look, had to see, had to know.

He moved to the brink of the hole. He looked down.

Then the breathing began.

In. Out. In. Out. It was a hoarse, rasping sound, very steady, very slow. Deep down in the sloping tunnel, just before it slanted out of sight among the building's foundations, something was moving furtively. Something as large as Jon, but sleek, slinkily lithe. Dark fur rippled in the dimness.

And among the fur, two ruby pinpoints lit up

like tiny, mean fires as a pair of alien eyes glinted up from the depths of the thing's dark lair.

At the sight of those eyes, the spell that had held Jon shattered and sanity smashed into his consciousness. He leaped back from the hole as a tide of terror and revulsion overtook him, then turned and ran.

If every rat in London had formed a wall to block Jon's way then, he would have torn them apart with his bare hands to get out of that place. He hurled himself across the room, and the next, and the next, and crashed through the door to the outside world to fall flat on his face on the platform.

As he hit the ground, he felt something clamp on his arm.

Jon screamed. His foot lashed out and he rolled over, punching with his free hand as he struggled to wrench his arm from his attacker's grip.

"Jon! *Jon!*"

The shout pierced through the red fog of Jon's terror, and his spinning mind realized the truth. It wasn't teeth sinking into his flesh, it was fingers. A human hand.

Dazed, he looked up and found himself staring into Frankie's eyes.

"Come on!" Frankie's face was grey. "Get up! Run! *Hurry!*"

He dragged Jon to his feet, and together they pelted to the bank. Frankie legged up first with Jon right behind him. Rubbish crunched and slithered under their feet, brambles tore at their arms and clothes, but they didn't care; all that mattered was to find the shortest, fastest way out of the cutting.

The trees that grew higher up gave them handholds. Reaching them, Jon had to stop. He couldn't breathe; his lungs and throat felt as if they were on fire, and he clung to a branch, doubled over, chest heaving.

"Come *on!*" Frankie yelled.

Jon choked out, "Hang on . . . Got to . . . rest . . . Be OK in a . . . minute. . ."

He heard Frankie slithering back down towards him, but his head was banging dizzily and he couldn't move. Then a new voice called out.

"Oi! You kids! What d'you think you're doing?"

Frankie froze, and Jon looked up blearily.

There was someone on the far side of the cutting: a man, wearing a hard hat and fluorescent orange safety waistcoat over denims. He must have come from further up the line, and he gestured angrily at them.

"You want to get yourselves killed? That's dangerous ground, you hear? Get out of there and stay out, or you'll be in trouble!"

Frankie stared back at the man.

"Dangerous. . ." he echoed. His face was twisted with bitterness. "He doesn't know what he's *talking* about! Serve him right if—"

He bit the words off. The man was standing with fists on hips, glaring, daring them to defy him. Frankie took hold of Jon's arm. "Come on," he said again.

Jon felt sick, but the dizziness was fading and he could breathe again. On leaden legs, he turned and dragged himself up the slope after Frankie.

9

They sat on the ground behind a bush, where no one could see them from the house. Frankie's face was tight and haggard, and there was despairing fear in his eyes, but he knew he had to talk. There was no other choice now.

"I don't know what it is," he said miserably. "I've never seen it properly; I just got a glimpse of it once." His gaze shifted sideways, nervously, to Jon's face. "It *can't* be a rat, not a real one. Real rats don't *get* that big. But. . ."

The words tailed off, and Jon nodded sombrely. He knew what Frankie meant. It

couldn't be a real rat, so it must be something
. . . *unreal*?

But unreal things couldn't bite you, could
they? Frankie's leg. His arm. That monstrosity
down there in the station was *real*, all right. It
existed. It was alive.

And it was *evil*.

"What happened to you?" he asked quietly.

Frankie brushed twitchily at his mouth. "It
was about a month ago," he said. "I was
exploring the station and I went into the old
building. I'd heard the stories about the dossers
and I was . . . curious, I suppose. Wanted to
see if I could find out what scared them off.
And I thought it might be a great place to go
and get away from everyone sometimes."

"I know," said Jon.

"Well, I got into the inner room. Where you
went? I was climbing around in there when I
heard this noise, like heavy breathing." He
stared at his own feet. "I should have got out
right then, but I didn't. I went to look. And
something bit me."

It was no more than a blur in the gloom,
Frankie went on, and it moved fast, lunging at
his leg and vanishing before he could get more

than a glance at it. Like Jon, he had run home, cleaned the wound and said nothing to anyone.

And like Jon, he had soon found that the bite wasn't healing, and other things were starting to happen.

"I have awful dreams," he said. "Every night. I dream something's calling to me, and I've got to go outside and down the cutting and back into that building. I can't stop myself. I know it's just a dream, but it scares the hell out of me."

Jon nodded again. He still couldn't remember his own nightmares, but he would have bet anything that they were along the same lines.

"Then I keep getting flashes of temper," Frankie added. "Really vicious. When they get bad I could *kill* someone. And animals hate me. You've seen that for yourself."

"It's happening to me, too," said Jon. "Gnasher won't come near me now – he growls and runs away."

"He would. But that's only the start of it, Jon. It gets worse. I've . . . I've had to start shaving. Not a beard or anything, but . . . fur. On my arms mostly, but it's growing round my mouth now, too; bristly, like whiskers."

A piece of puzzle slotted into place and Jon said, "The razor, and the hair in your bathroom basin. . ."

"You saw it, then? I thought so." A pause. "It hasn't started for you yet, I suppose?"

Jon shook his head. "The dreams and the bad temper and the animals, yes. But not that." His skin was prickling all over. "What else am I in for?"

Frankie hunched his shoulders. "Oh, plenty. Like finding yourself wanting to walk on all fours instead of upright. That's *not* funny, believe me! And then . . . things are happening to my mind – weird thoughts that don't make any sense. As if something's got hold of my brain and is *changing* it." He hesitated, then drew a deep breath, steeling himself for what he wanted to say.

"I'm not properly human any more, Jon. I'm turning into a rat. So are you. And – I don't think we're the first people it's happened to."

It was insane, Jon told himself. Any moment now he'd wake up and find that there was no monster rat, he wasn't changing and the whole thing had been a long, ugly nightmare.

But he only had to look at Frankie's miserable face to know that there wasn't going to be any awakening.

He understood why Frankie had refused to talk before. Who in their right mind would have believed him? Jon would have laughed out loud if he had been spun a story like that.

Until it happened to him, too.

And if Frankie's theory was right, they weren't the only ones.

"Remember I told you about the dossers?" Frankie said. "How they used to hang out in the old station?"

"Until three of them disappeared."

Frankie's lip curled. "Everyone *said* three, but who's to say that there weren't more? Six? A dozen? People don't care about the homeless, so who was counting?"

"You think they were . . . changed?"

"Looks likely, doesn't it?" Frankie gave Jon a sideways look that was unnervingly animal-like. "Some of those rats down there are *big*. You've seen them; you know. And they're clever. I'm not saying animals aren't intelligent; we know they are. But it's a different kind of intelligence to humans. Those rats, though. . ."

Jon remembered what had happened when he discovered the hole in the station house floor, just before *it* had bitten him. Those rats, gathering like a small, deadly army. The way they had stared at him, unafraid, not moving. The way they had started to close in. Jon was right: their intelligence seemed more human than animal.

So could they have *been* human, once?

"God!" he said. "That's *gruesome*. . ."

"Tell me about it." Frankie hunched his shoulders, as if he were suddenly cold. He wasn't going to like Jon's next question, but Jon had to ask it.

"Frankie . . . those nights when you were in the garden; when you dug up the rats that Gnasher had caught. Why did you do it?"

"I don't know," said Frankie. A frown crept over his face. "I can't remember what happened very clearly. I don't think I was properly awake; it was all like a dream."

"But what did you *do* with them?"

Frankie concentrated hard. "I *had* to dig them up," he said at last. "I remember that. It was as if there was this voice in my head, telling me – not in words but in another way I can't explain. It wanted me to take them home. Back to where they came from. So I went down the cutting, and. . ." His voice trailed off for a few moments, then: "I took them into the station building. Right inside, to that inner room. And I – I dropped them down the hole."

Into the thing's lair . . . Jon was baffled.

"What then?" he asked.

Frankie shook his head. "Nothing. I came out again and went home."

"That was all? The thing didn't attack you, or make you do anything else?"

"No. I didn't even see it. I just knew that I had to put the dead rats down there."

"So why did it want them? It doesn't make any sense! Unless – maybe it eats them?" Jon shuddered at the idea. "Maybe that's what it lives on: dead rats."

Frankie grimaced. "It's got to eat something, and I don't think it ever comes out of the station. Perhaps it uses its victims, controls them and makes them bring it food. . ."

Was that the cause of the dreams? Jon asked himself. Was the creature, whatever it truly was, reaching out, sliding into their thoughts and manipulating them?

"We've *got* to find out what that thing is," he said darkly.

Frankie sighed. "What's the point?"

"Don't be dumb! Unless we know what it is, how are we going to fight it?"

"Fight it?" Frankie echoed. "It's too late for that, Jon. Don't you understand? We're infected, we're changing, and there's nothing we can do!"

"There's a way to stop it!" Jon insisted. "There's *got* to be! We just have to find out how!"

Frankie laughed hollowly. "Oh, great! What d'you suggest we do – go back to that thing's lair and *ask* it, I suppose?"

There was silence for a moment as Jon stared at him. Then: "Yeah," he said. "Why not?"

10

"I must be out of my mind." Frankie stared at the darkening garden, his face tense and his eyes angry. "How did I let you talk me into this?"

"Well, you did, so stop whingeing about it. You can't back out now." In truth Jon was having enormous doubts of his own, but he wasn't about to admit it in case he lost his nerve altogether.

They were standing at the back door of the house. It was wet and blustery tonight, and the wind hissed in the trees beyond the garden wall with a sound like the sea surging.

"I still don't see why we can't leave it till morning," Frankie said. "Going down there after sunset – it's asking for trouble."

Jon sighed exasperatedly. "I told you, we haven't got any choice! That surveyor or whatever he was might be back tomorrow, and if he sees us he'll kick us out. Anyway, nothing ever happened to you when you took Gnasher's rats down there before, did it?"

"There's a first time for everything."

"Oh, shut up! Look, I'm not standing here arguing any more. Come or not, I don't care. But I'm going now."

Frankie hesitated, and for an awful moment Jon thought that he would say, "All right, you go," and walk back into the house. But after an indecisive second or two he sighed and nodded.

"OK. Come on, then. Let's get it over."

They made their way down the garden. The last light was fading from the sky and it was hard to see where they were going. But they dared not switch on their torches yet, in case anyone should look out of a window. They had told their parents that they were going to the cinema, so they'd have to make up some tale later about how good or bad the film had been.

If they got back in one piece. . .

Jon shivered at that thought and told himself firmly to stop being a prat. He was getting as jittery as Frankie – and anyway, what did they have to lose? Things could hardly get any worse.

He still didn't know whether what they were doing would achieve anything at all. Frankie thought it was completely demented, and now Jon was almost starting to agree with him. What could they learn at the station? He hadn't the least idea. But neither of them had come up with an alternative plan, and it had to be better – surely it did? – than giving up and doing nothing. Besides, in one sense the idea had been Frankie's in the first place. His scornful comment about "Going back to that thing's lair and asking it" had been the key. Not that they could actually "ask" it anything, of course. But by going to the underground lair together, they might discover something that would tell them exactly what they were up against.

The wind rose suddenly, blowing cold needles of rain into Jon's face and setting the trees roaring. Dimly ahead he could see the outline of the garden wall – then suddenly something tugged at his mind. Before he could stop himself he veered aside, towards a patch of overgrown shrubs.

"What the—" Jon stopped. He had to *make* himself stop. He stared at the bushes.

Then the tugging sensation came again. *Ahead. Under the bush. Look. You must. You must.*

"Jon?" Frankie had seen him and called softly. "What are you doing?"

Jon didn't know what he was doing. All he knew was that he *had* to look under those bushes.

He darted forward and dropped on to hands and knees, scrabbling among the wet leaves. He couldn't see a thing, but he *knew* something was there – something he must find.

He touched damp, cold fur, and his hand closed around the body of a rat and drew it out. For a moment he felt revolted. Gnasher had been at it again, only now he was hiding his kills where he thought they wouldn't be found.

Then the revulsion vanished and anger took its place. Anger with the cat, with all cats, and dogs, and humans, and—

"Jon!" Frankie spoke right by his shoulder,

and Jon jumped as though he had had an electric shock. "What are you—"

Then he stopped as he saw what Jon was holding. "Oh. . ." His voice sounded hollow.

"I've got to take it back, Frankie." Jon hardly recognized his own voice. "I've got to take it home."

"I know." Frankie shivered. "You haven't got any choice. That's how it was with me. Come on: let's not waste time."

Frankie moved on and Jon started to follow – then saw that Frankie had stopped again and was staring at him.

"What's the matter?" he said uneasily.

Frankie continued to stare. "Jon," he said, "try walking."

Jon looked down at himself and, to his horror, realized that he was still on all fours. He had been about to scuttle across the garden like an animal, because it hadn't occurred to him to stand up.

"Oh, no. . ." he groaned.

"Fight it!" Frankie urged. "Come on, Jon, get up! *Walk!*"

Jon did, but it was an effort, for something in his mind was trying to force him back to his hands and knees. At last Frankie grabbed his arm and hauled him up, and they hurried the last few metres to the wall. Over they went, Jon carrying the dead rat and suddenly finding it frighteningly easy to scramble and climb. They dropped into the cutting, switched on their torches and started off down the bank.

While from the garden, quick and quiet and invisible, several large, living rats scampered over the wall and ran after them.

In this dismal weather the abandoned station was creepier than ever. Rain hissed and pattered on the concrete platform, and everything had a chilly, wet sheen that made it spooky and unreal in the dusk.

The inside of the building was all too familiar to Jon now, but tonight the atmosphere was even more horrible. The rubble underfoot was sludgy-wet and slippery, and all around them was the desolate sound of water trickling and dripping. Neither of the boys wanted to lead the way, so they pressed side by side, moving their torches and sharply alert for any sign of movement.

"Whatever happens, keep together," Frankie

whispered. "And if you see or hear anything at all—"

"Don't worry, I'll yell!" Jon said fervently. He was still holding the rat, but the urgent pulling in his mind had faded; probably, he thought, because he was doing what *it* wanted him to do.

They reached the next room without any unpleasant surprises, and picked their way across to the inner door. Though neither of them said so aloud, they were both waiting for a sign that *it* was aware of their presence. But there was nothing – no sound, no furtive movement, no tingling sense of anything untoward in their minds.

Until they entered the third room and Frankie's torch beam reached the edge of the hole in the floor.

"*Uhh!*" Frankie jerked back as if he had been stung.

"What is it?" Jon hissed.

Frankie had recovered himself. "It's there," he whispered. "Under the floorboards. I can *feel* it."

Then Jon felt it, too. A waiting; an eagerness; and the faint pressure of alien thoughts crawling into his head. His fingers clenched and unclenched on the dead rat's body and, goaded by a force he couldn't control, he started to move towards the entrance of the lair.

Frankie, behind him, warned, "*Be careful!*" but the words seemed to come from a very long way off and they didn't mean anything to Jon. All he could think of was the task he must complete: to return Gnasher's prey to its proper place. To give it to. . .

To its master.

The knowledge came out of nowhere, and he was so shocked by it that he dropped the rat. Instantly a surge of fury blazed into his head: *Pick it up! Find it! Give me! Give me—*

"No, wait!" Jon cried out. "I'm looking for it, I'm looking!" Scrabbling frantically among the debris, he found the rat again – and immediately the fury vanished. Jon swore under his breath, and Frankie said,

"It's OK. I know what it's like. Just take the rat over to the hole."

Jon swallowed and nodded. Another couple of steps . . . Frankie's torch was shining directly into the creature's lair now; he could see the broken boards, the burrowed-out sides. . .

And something darker, bulkier, shifting restlessly deep, deep down.

"It's waiting," he murmured.

"I know. Go on; I'm right with you."

Jon nodded again. He reached the edge of the hole and paused, looking down. The thing had stopped moving, but he could feel it watching him. An instinct that wasn't his own said, *Yes, do it! Give it now!* but Jon fought it. Before he gave the creature what it wanted, he wanted something from it. And if its thoughts could invade his mind, then maybe it could work the other way round as well. . .

He thought savagely: *What are you?*

A flash of anger so furious that it physically hurt stabbed though Jon's skull. He yelped – and his hand started to move of its own accord. He tried to stop the movement, but he couldn't control his muscles. He was reaching out, over the hole, the rat dangling by its tail.

"Let it go!" Frankie shouted, as if he too was in pain. "For God's sake, just *drop* it!"

The rat fell from Jon's grasp and dropped with a *thump* to the bottom of the hole. What happened then was so swift, and so unexpected, that it caught Jon completely unawares. First there was a scuffling sound, and what looked like a huge shadow lunged from the depths of the hole, snatched the dead rat and darted back out of sight in one blurring movement. And secondly, as Jon's mouth opened in shock, a completely new sensation slammed into his mind.

For one hideous moment, Jon *became* the creature lurking down there under the old station. He saw with its eyes, he heard with its ears. He felt the alien muscles of its animal body, the warmth of its fur, the twitching of its whiskers sensing things beyond human reach. And he felt its emotions. Cunning. Greed. Hatred. Oh, it *hated* him and Frankie. They had dared to interfere with it, and it wanted revenge.

The realization of the revenge it would take flashed into Jon's head as clearly and violently as an explosion on a movie screen. His eyes widened, his jaw dropped – he flung a horrified glance at Frankie, and knew that Frankie had got the message, too.

They were the monster's prey. Slowly, surely, they were changing. And when they *had* changed, and were in its power, it intended to kill them.

11

"Baconburger and fries, cheeseburger and fries, two large Cokes." The girl behind the counter had strands of hair hanging down like rats' tails from under her paper baseball cap, and they made Jon shudder. She shoved the bag at them and they retreated to the quietest corner they could find.

"I don't want this," Frankie said, looking at his burger.

Jon scratched his face, which was itching. "Neither do I. But I'm going to try and eat it, because it might help me feel sane."

Rain was streaming down the burger bar's

windows. It was fully dark now and the street outside was just a blur of streaky lights and dim, hurrying movement. But the fact that there *were* lights and people out there made all the difference. It was the safe, real, familiar world, and right now Jon and Frankie needed that as they had never needed it before.

As the awful revelation flashed out of their minds again, the alien grip had vanished, too. Jon and Frankie didn't stop to say or do anything; they just ran. Pelting out of the station, they had half expected to hear the thing come crashing and slithering after them. It didn't, but they ran nonetheless, back up the bank, not stopping until they were in their own garden.

The burger bar had been Jon's idea. He couldn't face the thought of going home, and Frankie felt the same.

And they needed somewhere where they could talk.

Jon stuck a straw in his Coke and took a long drink, trying to get the awful taste of bile out of his mouth. He had to steel himself to speak.

"We both felt it, didn't we?" he said.

"Yeah," Frankie said tersely.

"Do you think it was real?"

Frankie frowned. "If you mean, did we imagine it or make it up, no. We can't have done; not both of us at exactly the same time."

Jon's face was still itching, and he had to force himself not to scratch it. "So how can that thing get into our minds? What *is* it – a mutant? A space alien? Where did it *come* from?"

Frankie didn't answer for a few seconds. Then: "I've been thinking about that. When the dossers started disappearing, there was that rumour about the weirdo who was supposed to have lived down there."

Jon remembered. "You said he died, but there was some talk about his ghost coming back."

"That's it. But it wasn't the only story that went around."

Jon tensed. "Tell me."

"Well . . . apparently he wasn't the typical loony wino. He didn't go round shouting and raving like they usually do; in fact he acted fairly sane most of the time. But there was this rumour that he was experimenting with something."

"What? In the station? You never told me that before!"

Frankie shrugged. "Didn't seem much point. I mean, it's crazy, isn't it? Really stupid. Who'd want to use a dump of a place like that for experiments? But now I've started wondering . . . what if the story's true?" He licked his lips nervously. "This was all years ago, when the railway line first closed, so I wasn't around, but I've heard all about it. And there's something else. The guy used to get through tons of dog and cat food. He stole it sometimes, from that shop on our corner; or he took half-finished tins and packets out of dustbins if people threw them away. Everyone thought he ate it himself. But what if he didn't? What if he was feeding something else? Something he kept secretly down there?"

"You mean he created the rat . . . like genetic engineering?" This was beginning to make a horrible kind of sense, Jon thought.

Frankie nodded. "When the guy died, he left his creation behind," he said softly. "And anyone it bites gets infected with a virus, or something, that turns them into rats, too."

"You said: 'when he died'," Jon put in. "What did he die of?"

There was a long silence. Then Frankie replied, "I don't think anyone knows. One day, people just noticed that he wasn't around any more. And he's never been seen since."

They were both thinking the same thing, but it was Jon who finally said it.

"So it might have been illness or old age. Or it might have been something else."

"Yeah," said Frankie. "It just might."

The mad scientist whose own creation turned on him – it was as far-fetched as the plot of an old horror movie. It was so ludicrous that it was funny. Only Jon and Frankie didn't feel like laughing.

Frankie was taking bits of gherkin out of his cheeseburger, then he changed his mind about eating it and put it down. "He could have been its first victim," he said hollowly. "Maybe it killed him. Or maybe it . . . changed him."

Then there were the dossers, Jon thought, *and its next target is us. . .*

He leaned across the table, his face white and strained. "Frankie, we've got to kill that thing!"

"Fine," Frankie said. "I agree. We'll napalm the station then, OK? Or if you've got a couple of SAM missiles kicking around your bedroom, that'd probably be less hassle. Or I'll get the Chieftain tank out of my wardrobe and—"

"Oh, shut up!" Jon interrupted angrily. "I get the point!"

"Good. Because we've got to come up with some *sensible* suggestions. Starting with. . ." Frankie stopped.

"What's up?" Jon asked uneasily.

Frankie's eyes had a peculiar, sombre look in them. "I think we'd better go, Jon. Now."

"Why?"

Frankie shoved his fries in one coat pocket and the box with the uneaten burger in the other. He stood up.

"Because," he said in a very low-pitched tone, "your face has just sprouted whiskers."

They ran all the way back home, Jon with his coat collar turned up and covering the lower half of his face. He could *feel* what was happening to him: the whiskers were only short and stubby as yet, but they pressed against the collar and made his mouth hurt.

By a stroke of pure luck, Frankie's parents were out. They let themselves into the downstairs flat, and Frankie hauled Jon straight to the bathroom.

"Get rid of them," he said. "Tweezers or my Dad's shaver; it doesn't matter which. There's the mirror, over there."

Jon turned his head away. He had started to shake. "I c-can't. . ." His eyes met Frankie's miserably. "I can't look. I don't want to see."

Frankie sighed. "You'll have to get over that eventually. I did. But OK; this time I'll do it for you. Let's try the tweezers."

Jon shut his eyes and clenched his teeth as Frankie pulled the whiskers out one by one. It hurt like anything, but he managed not to yelp too much. At last Frankie said, "That's the lot."

Jon rubbed his stinging face. "How long have I got before they grow again?" he asked unsteadily.

"No way of telling. It might be a few days, or a few hours. I suppose it depends on how fast the changes are happening to you." Frankie put the tweezers away and flushed the pulled-out whiskers down the loo. "With me, it's fur on my arms that's the biggest problem. I suppose everyone's different." He forced an unconvincing grin. "Shaving, at our age! Pretty crazy, isn't it?"

Jon tried to laugh, but couldn't, and after a second or two Frankie's false grin faded. "Come on," he said. "We left our Cokes at the burger bar, but there's some in the fridge."

Jon didn't want anything to eat or drink, but he trudged after Frankie to the kitchen. He felt unbearably depressed, and scared to the pit of his soul. Frankie had said, once before, that they couldn't fight this, and now Jon was beginning to agree with him. Fine, so now they had a good idea where the horror in the station had come from. But what good did that do? Knowing about it didn't tell them how to get rid of it, so what was the point in trying?

Frankie was pouring Coke into two large glasses and he handed one to Jon. Jon took it with a mumbled "Thanks", because it was less hassle than saying no, and trailed over to the window. He couldn't see far into the garden, but the kitchen light illuminated the concrete area around the dustbins.

And Gnasher.

The cat was sitting under the house's over-hang, where the rain couldn't reach him. He was washing himself, but suddenly, as though sensing Jon, he raised his head and looked straight at him.

His snarl wasn't audible through the window glass, but Jon felt it like a cold slap. Gnasher's fur bristled; he snarled again, then dashed away out of sight.

A wave of mingled fear and fury flashed through Jon's head, skidded round a mental corner and vanished. He found he was sweating, and with an enormous effort he got a grip on himself. For God's sake, that was *Gnasher*! His own cat. His *friend*! But just now, just for a moment, something had taken over his mind and made him *hate* Gnasher.

And that was something he wasn't about to tolerate!

"Frankie!" He turned from the window, and Frankie looked up in surprise at the sudden strength in his voice.

"What?"

Jon was angry, but it wasn't the vicious, alien anger of the mutant rat. This was a purely human feeling. He wasn't going to let his whole life be destroyed by this monstrosity!

"You made a joke earlier," he said to Frankie. "About napalm and missiles. OK; like

I said then, I get the point. But I don't believe that thing can't be killed."

Frankie watched him through narrowed eyes. "So. . .?"

"So we're going to try. You and me. We're going to fight back, Frankie. And we're going to win!"

12

"We could shoot it," Jon said. "Or poison it. They're the two most obvious ways."

They were sitting in Frankie's bedroom; Frankie on the bed, hunched and brooding, Jon on the floor with his legs sprawled out in front of him.

"Shooting's no good," Frankie stated morosely. "We haven't even got an airgun between us, and not a hope in hell of getting one. And even if we could get one, what use do you think it would be against that thing? It'd take a high-powered rifle, minimum, to do it any damage."

He was right, Jon admitted to himself. "Well, what about poison, then?"

"Same problem," said Frankie. "Yeah, we could go and buy some rat killer or whatever, but how much effect would it have? That thing is *not* an ordinary animal; it could probably eat half a tonne of the stuff and not even get indigestion." He paused. "And that could give us some real problems."

"What do you mean?"

"Think about it. We try to kill it, and it doesn't work. Result: one very aggravated giant rat. And I wouldn't want to be around when it came looking for us."

A small, cold shiver went down the length of Jon's spine.

Frowning, he said, "There are stronger things than rat poison."

"Sure there are; much stronger. But one, how do we get hold of them, and two, would they work either? We don't know. I don't think we can afford to take the risk."

Jon nodded glumly. He could have argued that Frankie was a defeatist, but truthfully there wasn't any point. Frankie wasn't being a defeatist; he was being sensible. Anything they did would have to be a sure-fire certainty, or it was too dangerous.

The trouble was, they had gone over all the possibilities they could think of, and they were getting nowhere. They'd thrown out all the really ludicrous thoughts, like vats of acid or flamethrowers, and narrowed the possibilities down to several that were at least feasible. Now, though, Jon saw that the ideas they had left would probably have about as much effect on their enemy as a chihuahua against a rottweiler. The grim truth was that they were up against something too weird, and too powerful, to combat.

They both looked up at the sound of the flat door opening, and Frankie's face fell. "That's Mum and Dad," he said.

Jon looked at his watch and groaned. "I'll have to go, or we'll both get nagged about it being so late."

As if on cue, the bedroom door opened and Frankie's dad looked in. "Hello, you two. Good film?"

"Not bad," Frankie said.

"I'd have thought you'd be in bed by now. You too, Jon. Do you know what time it is?"

"I'm just going, Mr Lambert," said Jon.

"OK. I don't want your parents thinking we're getting you into bad habits. 'Night, then."

He closed the door and Jon pulled a face at it. "I'd better get back." He got up and started across the room. "We'll get together again tomorrow, right?"

"Right." Frankie's face twitched, as if he was going to sneeze.

"See you."

"Yeah. See you."

As Jon went out, he saw Frankie raise one hand and brush quickly at his mouth.

And he also saw the soft down of grey-brown fur growing on Frankie's arms and hands.

The noise started at eight o'clock the next morning.

Jon woke with a start and sat up in bed, wondering fuzzily what the racket was. Then he recognized it. A chainsaw – and not very far away. What on earth. . .?

He got up and went to the window, pulling the curtains back. For a moment or two he

113

couldn't imagine where the noise was coming from, but then he saw one of the tallest trees beyond the garden wall start to shake.

Whatever was going on, it was going on in the railway cutting.

Jon grabbed his clothes. He was half-way through dressing when, suddenly and un-pleasantly, he remembered what had happened to him last night. Heart thumping, he touched the skin of his face. He couldn't feel anything, but. . .

It took all his nerve to make himself turn and look in the small mirror on his wall. When he did, though, relief swept over him. There was nothing wrong – no fur, no whiskers, no changes.

At least, not yet.

Trying not to think about that, Jon threw on the rest of his clothes and headed for the front door. As he passed the kitchen, Mum called out to him.

"Jon? You're up early!"

"The saw woke me," Jon said. "What's going on?"

"I've no idea. Though if they're getting rid of those trees, I won't grumble. They cut so much sunlight out of the garden." She held up a packet of cereal. "Want some breakfast?"

"In a minute," Jon said. "I'm just going downstairs."

"Don't go near that chainsaw!"

Don't worry, Jon thought. *I'm not going anywhere near the cutting unless I absolutely have to!*

Opening the door to the garden, he found Frankie there before him. Frankie looked pale and had his T-shirt on inside out. There was a new red shaving rash on his arms.

"You heard it, then," he said, nodding towards the cutting.

"I'd have to be deaf or dead not to." Jon narrowed his eyes. "What're they doing?"

"Felling trees and clearing some of the undergrowth. There's a JCB down there, though God knows how they got it in."

"Why are they doing it?"

"I don't know." Frankie hunched his shoulders. "They've been talking about redeveloping ever since the line shut, so maybe this is it."

They were both thinking the same thing, and Jon voiced it. "So what's going to happen to the station?"

Frankie looked at him, then said again, "I don't know. But if they knock it down. . ."

"Yeah. If they knock it down, what's our friend in there going to do then?"

The thought that the old station building might be demolished was like a slap of cold water shaking the boys out of their gloom. As Jon said, it didn't actually *change* anything, but it opened up a whole new set of possibilities. And it wasn't long before they fixed on one possibility in particular.

Looking over the garden wall, they saw the tree-cutters: two men in goggles, ear-muffs and bright yellow safety helmets. They had already cleared quite a few of the young saplings away, and now they were starting work on some of the larger trees. The chainsaws screamed and whined with a noise that set Jon's teeth on edge, then with a groan one of the largest trees keeled over and crashed down among the undergrowth. Through the gap it left Jon saw the JCB. It was down on the station platform, looking like a sort of techno-dinosaur among the shabby brick and concrete. It wasn't doing anything, but three more men were standing near it, talking. One was the man who had shouted at them the other day; another was setting up what looked like measuring equipment.

"They must have brought the digger along the railway track somehow," Jon said, craning to see better.

Frankie wasn't really listening, because suddenly he spoke.

"Jon . . . can you feel anything?"

"Feel anything?" Jon was baffled.

"In your head." Frankie turned and looked at him. "I can. A kind of . . . stirring." He licked his lips nervously. "I'm getting angry. And I'm getting worried."

Jon tensed, then he felt it too. A surge of awareness that wasn't his own but came from outside him. Anger, yes. Suspicion. Doubt.

And the beginnings of fear.

It was reacting to the disturbance. And it didn't like what was happening one bit.

Jon shut his eyes tightly and tried to force the alien feelings away. He needed a clear head now as never before. If the monstrous creature's mind took him over, he'd run screaming and shouting into the cutting, attack the workmen, go completely crazy.

"*Get out, get out!*" He hissed it aloud without realizing, and Frankie said, "Fight it, Jon! We've got to!"

Then, as suddenly as it had come, the feeling vanished. Jon reeled back from the wall with a gasp and bent double – *No, you don't want to go on all fours! You don't! You don't!* – until his breath came back.

When he looked up, Frankie was watching him, and there was an excited light in his eyes.

"It's cornered, Jon," he said, "and it knows it. It's not going to hang around there much longer – it's going to have to come out into the open. And if those guys see it. . ."

This could be the answer they had been praying for. "If they see it, they'll have to do something," Jon said softly.

"Too right they will!" Frankie nodded, a slow smile spreading across his face. "We haven't got a way to kill that rat, Jon." His gaze swivelled meaningfully towards the cutting. "But *they* have. . ."

13

Jon and Frankie hadn't bargained for the monstrous rat's reaction to the upheaval in the cutting.

It hit Frankie first, as a burst of the filthiest temper he had ever had. Twice, Jon had to forcibly stop him from charging into the cutting and launching a furious attack on the workmen, and the second time Frankie actually bit him in an attempt to make him let go. The temper faded after a while – maybe when the rat realized that the tactic wasn't going to work – but it left both boys feeling drained and exhausted.

Then there was trouble with Gnasher. Jon didn't want the cat getting in the cutting, so he kept him indoors. Gnasher, though, had other ideas, and tried every trick he knew to escape. He was wildly excited, pacing the flat with lashing tail and bristling fur, and whenever Jon tried to go near him he hissed and spat ferociously. By lunchtime Jon's hands were covered in scratches and Gnasher had gone to ground under the sofa, from where he continued to grumble and swear.

After lunch, Frankie came up to the flat and the boys retreated to Jon's room. The chainsaws were still working; the noise grated in their ears, and by mid-afternoon they were getting very jumpy. Jon was horribly aware of the monstrous rat's lurking presence in the back of his mind. It was getting more and more agitated. It couldn't be much longer before it decided to *do* something.

They spent the afternoon trying to distract themselves with computer games. Outside, the sky was getting heavier and darker, and by five o'clock there was an ominously oppressive stillness in the air.

"Going to be a storm," Frankie said, looking

up from the screen.

Jon shivered. He wasn't willing to admit it, but he didn't like storms. It was the lightning, not the thunder, that put the wind up him. Thunder was just a noise, but lightning was dangerous. He'd seen this film on TV once, where someone took shelter under a tree and—

Oh, shut up! he told himself savagely. As if he didn't have enough problems, without letting this scare him as well. It was only a bit of grubby sky. There probably wouldn't even *be* a storm.

It seemed he was right, because by the time he went to bed there hadn't been so much as a drop of rain. The oppressiveness hadn't gone, though, and his bedroom was stifling. Jon lay awake for a long time. He could hear Gnasher in the hall: the cat was prowling about, uttering an occasional "*rrrow!*" of frustration as he tried to get out through the front door. The noise irritated Jon, and he had to hold on to his temper. He was so hot! His skin itched. He wanted to throw something. He wanted to kick something. He wanted to *bite*. . .

Suddenly he sat up with a flurry of bed-clothes, and as he did so, the echoes of a dream skittered from his mind. Confused, Jon looked at his watch. Gone two? He must have fallen asleep after all.

God, the room was stifling! He could hardly breathe; there didn't seem to be any air left in the whole world. And the dream . . . he could dimly remember it, and it disturbed him. Something had been nagging at his brain, calling to him.

Calling. . .

Jon's body jolted suddenly, as if he had had an electric shock. At the same instant something grabbed at his mind, gripped it, and a red haze swam over his vision. Before he knew it he was out of bed and fumbling towards the door.

No! a desperate voice inside him tried to scream. *No, stop it! I won't! You can't make me!* But it was a lost voice. He couldn't control himself. Something else had taken over – something that wasn't human.

He found himself at the door, but when he tried to turn the doorknob he couldn't make his hands work properly. They didn't seem to be hands any more; they felt more like . . . more like *feet*. . .

Then by sheer chance he did something right, and the door swung open. Jon scurried out into the hall. *Front door, stairs, garden –* it was all he could think of. Had to get *out* of here! Had to *go!*

He didn't see Gnasher crouching in the living-room doorway, but Gnasher saw him. The cat watched wide-eyed as Jon scuttled on all fours up the hall. A soft growl rose in his throat as Jon pawed and clawed at the front door until, at last, he got it open. And as Jon scampered out like a huge, clumsy rat, Gnasher flattened himself low to the floor and started to slink after him.

Jon came to his senses to find himself crouching on hands and knees, barefoot and wearing his pyjamas, in the middle of the garden. His mouth dropped open in a round "O" of shock, and as he started to scramble to his feet an urgent voice hissed his name.

He jumped and spun round. Frankie was behind him.

"Frankie. . ." Jon felt confused and dizzy. "I had this dream. I woke up, and then. . ." His voice tailed off as he saw that Frankie, too, was wearing pyjamas, and realized what it meant. "You, as well?" he asked.

Frankie nodded. "I couldn't stop myself. Something was pulling me and I had to come out here." He looked towards the cutting. "*It*'s on the move, Jon."

Jon's eyes were adjusting to the night now, and by the wall he saw movement. "Look!" he whispered, pointing. "Over there."

Small shapes were scurrying around the wall. One after another they scrabbled up and over, vanishing with the faintest of rustles into the tangle beyond.

"Rats. . ." Frankie said. "It's disturbed them, too. It's going to move out of the station; it's going to look for somewhere new. We've got to find out where it's going!"

Jon shivered. "All right." He looked down at himself. "Can you get dressed and get out again without waking anyone?"

"Should be able to."

"OK. Meet you back here. And bring your torch!"

Five minutes later they were both in the garden again. Everything was uncannily quiet, muffled by the heavy, humid night. Even when they climbed over the wall and dropped down into the vegetation, their feet hardly seemed to make any sound.

Frankie shone his torch around. "Half the trees have gone already."

"I know. And the JCB's still by the platform. Looks like they're going to start demolishing the station pretty soon."

Something rustled by their feet and skimmed away ahead of them, making Jon jump.

"More rats," Frankie muttered under his breath. "How many *are* there round here?"

"If they're all going where I think they are, I expect we'll soon find out," Jon said.

They started to climb carefully down the slope. Behind and above them, Gnasher crouched on the garden wall, staring intently at their progress. A few moments later he was joined by a second cat – the big tabby from a few doors away. Normally, Gnasher and the tabby were deadly enemies. Tonight, though, things were different, and within another minute several more cats had appeared silently out of the night. Two black-and-white females, a black tom, a big, thuggish ginger with a torn ear . . . and more. Many more. They all took their places on the wall. They all watched.

Then, as though some strange, telepathic communication had passed between them, they slipped stealthily down into the cutting.

14

"Did you feel that?" Frankie whispered. "Rain."

Jon was relieved that it wasn't something spookier. But rain might mean that the storm was going to break, and that didn't help his nervousness one bit.

Far in the distance a long, slow train rattled along a track. The wheels made a desolate sound that seemed to match Jon's thudding heart: Clack-clack, clack-*clack* . . . clack-clack, clack-*clack*. . . He wished they hadn't come. He wished he was back indoors, in bed, asleep. Even his nightmares would be better than this. At least with nightmares you woke up eventually.

They had reached the platform, and Frankie was moving cautiously towards the station building. They hadn't seen any more rats, which worried Jon. Where were they all? He'd half expected the platform to be alive with them, but there was nothing here at all.

Frankie reached the broken-down door and looked back. "Come on!" he hissed.

Jon followed reluctantly. They shone their torches in through the door. Nothing. A spot of rain fell on Jon's hand. If the storm was starting. . .

The thought made him want to get out of the open, and he pushed Frankie aside and went into the station.

Inside, he stood very still, listening and watching. It was too quiet. There wasn't a sound or a twitch of movement. Joining him, Frankie whispered, "Weird, isn't it? Let's go through."

They squeezed through the next door. The scene was the same: not a flicker of anything. Jon started to murmur, "Where are the—" but before he could finish, Frankie's hand gripped his arm.

"*Over there!*"

"There" was the gap into the third and last room, where something *was* moving.

As the torch beams shone in, they saw them: a tide of rats, scrabbling and jostling on the floor of the innermost room. They looked like a living, writhing carpet, and though none of them was uttering a single squeak, their feet and bodies made an eerie *hush-swishing* sound.

"*Ugh!*" Frankie backed away from the door. The rats had taken no notice of the torches, but at the sound of his voice, their movement stopped instantly. For one second there was absolute silence and stillness. Then, very slowly, every rat in the room turned its head and looked at the boys.

Time seemed to crawl to a halt as Jon and Frankie stared back at the rats. Those eyes – hundreds and hundreds, each one a tiny, mean, red pinpoint. He wanted to turn and run but he couldn't make his legs move.

"Jon," Frankie said in a small, terrified voice, "it's here. It's been waiting. It's calling to me. . ."

Then Jon felt it, too. The tugging in his mind. The command he had to obey. *Come to*

me. I want. I need. Come to me. Come
HERE!

"No. . ." He struggled to get the word out
through gritted teeth, fighting the pull with all
his strength. His foot slid back. It wasn't going
to control him! He was going, he was getting
out of here!

Something pressed against the back of his
leg. Jon whipped round, the torch swinging.

The rats. They were crowding in the doorway, climbing on and over each other to block
the boys' escape route. Their eyes glared
malevolently. They showed their teeth, small
but vicious.

And the alien voice in Jon's head said:
COME HERE!

Frankie made a dreadful moaning noise. The
torch fell from his hand and he dropped to all
fours, his body shuddering. Then, to Jon's
horror, he began to crawl across the floor,
towards the gaping hole, and *its* lair.

"Frankie, don't!" Jon yelled. But Frankie had
forgotten him. Frankie had forgotten everything except the hideous summons. He was
obeying. He had no other choice.

Jon tried to reach Frankie. But the rats,

which had parted to let Frankie through, closed in again, and Jon's legs were enveloped in a scrambling, scrabbling mass of furry bodies. They ran at him, leaped at him, driving him back until he stumbled hard against the wall.

Frankie crawled on. He reached the hole in the floor. A piece of roof-timber had fallen across it, and Frankie tried to drag it clear.

"Jon, help me!" His voice didn't even sound human. "Got to – shift it – *got* to!" He hauled at the timber, muscles straining. Suddenly the beam moved and rolled aside. Dust billowed up in a thick cloud as it hit the floor.

The cloud began to clear, and Jon saw the dark, menacing bulk that was heaving itself out of the underground lair.

He had never come face to face with it before this moment, and the horrible reality froze him rigid. Its body was as big as his own, and covered with dense, matted fur. Its tail was as thick as a hawser, lashing in the dust. Its head, ugly and misshapen, hung low, menacing below the muscular shoulders. Its eyes, red-rimmed and burning like coals, were fixed on him with malignant, greedy hatred.

They were human eyes.

Jon felt the strength going from his arms and legs. He tried to hold on to his torch, but his fingers were numb and he couldn't control them. The torch crashed to the floor and went out, and darkness engulfed the room.

And in Jon's petrified mind, something commanded: *HERE. TO ME. NOW!*

He felt the small rats around him stir eagerly. He felt them scurry out of the way as his feet began to move. Towards the monstrosity. Towards those glaring, waiting eyes.

He didn't hear the new and violent hiss of rain on the ground outside. But the second noise – the sudden, unexpected commotion of shrieks and squeals from the outer room – shocked him out of his paralysis. The spell in his mind shattered as he heard the monstrous rat give a furious snarl.

Then the first lightning flash blazed through the station, and in its blinding glare Jon saw the cats.

There must have been at least twenty of them, and they were attacking the rats in a scything mayhem of teeth and claws. Thunder rumbled like the crack of doom, and a second flash lit up a seething mass of bodies as the rats tried frantically to escape. Squeaking their terror, they poured towards doors and windows in a scrambling, tumbling river. The cats were wreaking havoc, and in the light of a third lightning flash Jon saw Gnasher, wild-eyed and excited in the middle of it all.

And Gnasher saw Jon. He stopped, staring, a dead rat pinned down under his front paws. Lightning shivered through the room again and Gnasher looked beyond Jon. His body tensed – and raising his head, he gave a piercing, yowling cry.

The sound made Jon jump as much as the lightning had done. But its effect on the monstrous rat was more shocking still. A violent scuttering noise gave Jon an instant's warning before a dark shape smeared across his vision and the rat streaked past, knocking him aside as it bolted for the doorway.

It barrelled through the gap – and straight into the waiting ambush.

Gnasher's cry had been a signal, and every cat in the building launched itself into an all-out attack on the monster. Jon heard its scream of rage and pain as they fell on it, and in the next flare of lighting he saw it writhing under their onslaught. They were on its back, slashing at its head now. Six of them clung scrabbling and clawing to one of its back legs, and another four had seized its tail. The rat shrieked again, and Jon yelled, too, in a kind of awful exultation: "Get it, Gnasher! Get it!"

But though the rat was outnumbered, it still had size and strength on its side. Its tail whipped suddenly, throwing the clinging cats off. Then with a huge, wrenching twist it broke free and charged for the outside door.

Jon didn't pause to think; he plunged in its wake, through the next room and into the old ticket office. He was in time to see the rat smash through the door and vanish, with the last of the surviving small rats on its heels. He expected the cats to follow, but they didn't. Suddenly, they were still.

They were all looking at him, as if they expected him to do something.

"Jon, come on!" Frankie came stumbling from behind him. He had retrieved his torch and it was still working. "We can't let it get away!"

Jon's mind was spinning and he was too breathless to answer, but Frankie didn't wait.

He ran to the door and disappeared outside.

"Frankie?" Jon croaked. Then he thought: *if the rat gets away, if it vanishes in the night, we might never find it again.*

And their only hope would vanish with it.

"Frankie!" Like a swimmer launching into deep water Jon pushed his aching legs into action and lurched towards the door. "Frankie, wait for me!"

15

Running through the storm was like the maddest dream Jon had ever had. The rain bucketed down, driving in his face and soaking his clothes and hair, and the lightning was almost continuous. He had no time to worry about that now – so much had happened to him, so much that was completely and utterly insane, that a thunderstorm was nothing!

Frankie saw him coming and waited for him under the old iron bridge along the railway track, out of the rain. Slithering to a halt, John gasped, "This is useless! It can run much faster than us; we'll never keep up!"

For answer, Frankie pointed the torch down the track and said, "Look."

At the limit of the beam, through a veil of falling water, Jon saw the rat. It had given up any idea of trying to control the boys; all it could think of now was getting away. It was fleeing along the line and had almost reached the curve – but it was moving slowly, hobbling, as if every step was a painful effort.

"The cats must have hurt its leg pretty badly," Frankie said. "It can't run far; it'll look for somewhere to hide. Come on, Jon – this is the only chance we'll get!"

Jon didn't need telling twice. Frankie had already started off along the track again, and he followed.

The rat had disappeared round the curve, but as the boys emerged from under the bridge they saw it again, limping ahead of them. It kept hesitating, looking from side to side as if searching for a bolt-hole. But the cutting here was lined with brick walls on either side and there was no escape; it could only go on.

Jon and Frankie ran side by side down the middle of one of the tracks, jumping from sleeper to sleeper. Lightning funnelled through the cutting again, followed by an echoing bawl of thunder, and Jon had awful visions of a train looming suddenly out of the murk. Above the din he called out, "Frankie! Are you *sure* this line's abandoned?"

"Yes!" Frankie yelled back. "It was shut years ago!"

"All the same—"

"Look, it's *OK*!" Frankie slowed down and gestured ahead. "See those points, where the other track crosses over? That leads to a line that *is* still used, but it's twenty or thirty metres away from this one. Nothing's going to hit us, so keep going!"

They ran on. The wooden sleepers were greasy underfoot and twice Jon slipped, the second time falling flat and grazing his hands and knees in the gravel ballast. Frankie stopped to help him to his feet – then as he straightened up again, he tensed.

"What's up?" Jon shouted.

"Where's it gone?" Frankie swung the torch, but the rain was so heavy now that everything was a blur. "I can't see it!"

Dismay punched through Jon. Up ahead

where the lines crossed, the railway tracks looked like a tangle of giant steel spaghetti, but the rat's limping, waddling shape had disappeared.

"It was there a moment ago!" Wildly, Frankie looked from side to side. "It can't have climbed up the bank! Where *is* it?"

Then Jon glimpsed a flicker of movement. "There!" he cried.

Frankie saw it. It had scrambled over the points and was on the other track, where it curved away to join the working line.

"Come on!" Frankie yelled. "We've got to catch up!"

The chase began again. Where the two lines joined, the cutting was deeper, rising almost vertically to another bridge with rows of houses on one side and a main road on the other. Jon heard a lorry drone by on the road. He could hardly believe that they were only a few metres away from the real, sane world.

"Come *on!*" Frankie shouted again.

Jon forgot sanity and raced after him.

The rat wasn't far ahead, and it was definitely slowing down. But they were nearing the working part of the railway now, and that meant hiding places: arches, huts, three open wagons in a siding. . . If they lost their quarry in this maze, they'd never find it again.

Then, with a titanic *crack*, a lightning bolt seared across the sky. For an instant the world was blotted out by the flash, and Jon's yelp of fright was drowned by bellowing thunder. Frankie dropped the torch in shock; it rolled and stopped several metres away, its beam pointing uselessly back the way they had come.

Cursing himself, Frankie went to retrieve the torch. But when he shone it along the line again, the rat was nowhere to be seen.

"It's got away!" There was stark anguish in Frankie's voice.

Jon came to stand beside him, trying to ignore the fact that he was shaking with fear. "It must be round here somewhere," he said desperately.

"Oh, sure. But where do we start looking?"

A peculiar sensation prickled in the back of Jon's mind. He didn't recognize it at first; he had forgotten all about it. But it came again, more strongly. His mouth twitched. His skin began to itch. And suddenly he had an over-powering urge to look over his shoulder. . .

Very, very cautiously, he turned round.

And saw it.

It was no more than five paces away. It crouched on the track, and by the glow of the distant street lamps he could see the crimson glare of its eyes.

And something was crawling into his mind, tugging at him, commanding him. . .

"Frankie. . ." Jon said in a low, quavering voice.

Frankie looked. He froze, and slowly the rat turned its head until it was staring straight at him. Jon heard Frankie's gasp, saw him step back. Then he stopped. His fingers flexed: for a moment he tried to fight the compulsion, but then his hand opened and the torch dropped to the ground.

"No. . ." Frankie whispered. "No, I – I won't!"

The rat's bulk shifted menacingly. It shuffled towards him, and Jon felt the pressure in his head, the ugly, animal thought that said: *I am hungry. I need strength. I need your strength. . .*

The monstrosity was sapping Frankie's will, stealing energy from his mind. Frankie was hypnotized. He couldn't move or speak. It was controlling him, and it was going to use him to save itself.

Jon's foot slid back. The rat ignored him. It had Frankie, and one victim was enough – for now.

Another step back. Still the rat took no notice. Frankie's hands came jerkily up and he brushed at his mouth, like an animal brushing its whiskers. He whimpered, and the sound was like a squeak. Then he dropped to his knees, to all fours. And he started to crawl, slowly, towards the waiting rat.

Something snapped in Jon's mind. He whirled round, snatched up the fallen torch and shone it straight into the rat's face. The thing recoiled with a squeal and suddenly Jon was yelling at it, his voice rising to a screech like the yowl of a fighting cat.

A fighting cat. . .

The rat shrieked with fury and fear, and in a blaze of inspiration Jon slammed all his mental energy into the thought that he *was* a cat. *Cat! Cat! Bite you, claw you, attack you, hate you! Cats hurt you, and I'm a cat, as big as you! Cat, cat, CAT!*

He yowled again, and the rat turned tail and

ran. With a snarl, Jon was after it. He could feel it scrabbling in his mind, fighting him, trying to overcome him, but he threw the images of *CAT* at it, chasing it down the line like Gnasher chasing his prey. The rat was staggering, weaving from side to side; it stumbled over another set of points and tottered on with Jon in pursuit.

Jon heard Frankie's high-pitched cry of warning, but its meaning didn't register until suddenly the track under his feet started to vibrate. A heavy rumbling . . . the whining drone of a big diesel motor . . . and, echoing in the cutting, the relentless *clack-clack . . . clack-clack* of steel wheels on steel rail.

The train appeared round the curve like a huge, slow-moving serpent, looming out of the darkness with its headlights glaring and flickering. Jon heard the labouring beat of the engine, heard the long train of wagons clanking behind – and saw the rat, still running, heading for the working line.

He skidded to a stop, and the rat stopped too. It looked back. The red coals of its eyes glittered.

With all his willpower Jon thought: *CAT!*

The rat fled.

Straight into the path of the oncoming train.

The engine driver didn't even glimpse it, because it ran under the beam of the headlights as the big diesel toiled unstoppably on. There was no awful sound, no thump, no squeal. The rat just disappeared beneath the turning wheels, and the train continued on its ponderous way.

Jon stood motionless, watching as the wagons went by. The last one passed and with a flicker of red tail-lights the train faded into the distance. Still Jon didn't move. The rain was lessening and the lightning had stopped. He had switched the torch off, though he couldn't remember doing it, and everything seemed very, very dark. And very, very unreal.

Then a footstep scrunched in the ballast behind him.

"I saw it. . ." Frankie's voice was unsteady.

"Yeah. . ." Jon couldn't think of anything else to say. They were silent for a few seconds.

"Give me the torch, Jon." Frankie reached out and took it from him.

"Why?" Jon asked. "What are you—"

"I've got to make sure. Make sure it's really dead."

Jon's stomach turned over at the thought. He wanted to argue, but something in Frankie's tone made him stop. Frankie switched on the torch and started to walk across the line, and after a moment Jon swallowed his squeamishness and followed.

There was a dark shape lying on the track. Jon hesitated, but Frankie walked steadily on. He reached the shape. He shone the torch down.

"Jon. . ." he said softly.

Jon steeled himself to look. The rat was a horrible mess, its body so crushed that he felt a sick lurch at the sight of it. But its head was intact. The eyes stared upwards, seeing nothing, and the mouth hung slackly open.

And its face wasn't a rat's face.

It was a man's. An old man, with a ragged beard and glazed, fanatical eyes.

Jon recoiled, his own eyes bulging. Then the face of the dead creature changed. Fur and long whiskers replaced the beard. The eyes grew small, red. The mouth altered its shape and the long incisor teeth reappeared. It was a rat again.

But for one uncanny moment, it had been human.

The boys looked at one another. Jon began, "But. . ." and couldn't get any further.

Frankie swallowed. "We didn't see that," he whispered. "We *can't* have done. . ."

Jon was silent. Part of him was trying desperately to believe that Frankie was right. It had been a trick of the torchlight, that was all.

But another part of him believed something else entirely. The weirdo who had lived in the station, the experimenter, the madman – mad enough to have turned himself into a monster. . .

But things like that weren't possible. Were they?

A peculiar, cold light flickered suddenly over the corpse. For a moment Jon saw the outline of the track through it . . . and then it began to fade. Its outlines grew vaguer, until, like smoke drifting away, it vanished, leaving only a strange, dark smudge, like an oil-stain, on the line.

Jon put his hands over his face and sucked in a harsh breath. He felt Frankie grip his arm, and he tried to say, "What was—"

"I don't know," Frankie interrupted. "I don't suppose we ever will." He stared down at the empty rail. "Does it matter?"

It did – and yet in another, bizarre way it didn't. The thing – human or animal or whatever it truly was – was dead, and they were alive.

At least. . .

Jon took the torch from Frankie. He pushed his sleeve up and shone the beam on his right arm, where the sticking plaster was. The skin around it was no longer red. He tore the plaster off. It hurt, but there was no wound, not a mark, nothing.

Frankie saw. "It's gone. . ." he said. He didn't need to look at his leg; he knew what he would find. "Oh, God, Jon!" Suddenly there was a catch in his voice. "We're *safe!*"

The rain had stopped as they walked slowly back along the disused line. Neither of them said a word on the way; they couldn't, because nothing they could have said would make any sense.

The old station was empty and silent. It felt weird to climb up on the platform and walk past the building. Jon kept expecting to see rats, but none appeared. He doubted if they would ever go back there again. The JCB reared up against the sky, and Frankie patted it. "Go for it, mate!" he said. "Knock it all down. Sooner the better."

They climbed wearily up the bank and over the garden wall. The house was in darkness, but something moved in the bushes. Then a small shape appeared.

"Mrrowr?" said Gnasher. He came up to Jon and rubbed hard against his legs, then turned his attention to Frankie, who bent down and stroked him.

"He likes me," Frankie said wonderingly. "And I'm not scared of him any more. . ."

Jon picked up the cat, who started to purr smugly. "Course he likes you," he said, and though his grin was shaky, it *was* a grin. "I told you before, didn't I? Gnasher loves people."

"But rats. . ." Frankie said.

"Yeah. Not rats." The grin faded and Jon looked back to the wall and tangle of the cutting beyond. "Never, *ever* rats."

Are they ordinary animals – or are they

Creatures ...?

Don't miss

Who's Been Sitting in My Chair?

by Louise Cooper

Turn the page and read on

Creatures – you have been warned!

Rhoda and her parents had had quite enough of house-straightening for one day, and were watching television in the sitting room, with their dinners on their laps. Mum and Dad were on the sofa, while Rhoda sat in the old armchair. Opal still wouldn't come near the chair, so for once Rhoda was able to eat a meal without the Siamese cat patting her leg with a paw and noisily demanding her share. When everyone had finished Rhoda took the plates out to the kitchen, then returned to settle down and watch what looked as if it might be a good thriller. Dad was half asleep, and Mum kept a vague eye on the screen while she was doing a crossword, and after a time Rhoda began to feel deliciously drowsy. She closed her eyes, though still listening to the film – then she sensed a presence nearby, and a moment later felt the unmistakable weight of Opal jumping on to her lap.

"Hiya, puss," she said lazily. Opal settled comfortably, and Rhoda felt pleased that she'd finally got over her sulks and decided to give the chair a try. Eyes still shut, she reached out a hand to stroke the cat's fur.

There was nothing there but her own knees.

Rhoda's eyes started open and she stared at the empty space where Opal should have been. This was insane! She could *feel* the Siamese, as surely and solidly as she could feel herself – yet Opal wasn't anywhere in sight!

Rhoda looked wildly towards the sofa, her mouth opening to blurt to Mum and Dad. Then the sound caught and jammed in her throat as she saw her cat. Opal was on the sofa's middle cushion, wedged between her parents and stretched out to full length with her head on her front paws. She looked lazy and relaxed – but her blue eyes were open, and glaring with a fixed, brilliant stare at Rhoda's legs.

She was watching something. And the invisible weight on Rhoda's lap tensed and shifted, as if that same something was glaring straight back.

Goosebumps

R.L. Stine

Reader beware, you're in for a scare!

These terrifying tales will send shivers up your spine: